CW00433972

This boo
shown be
required
or teleph
on the la

HIGH
WYCOMI
LIBRARY
BOOK
RENEWAL
TEL:- 0149
471862

L.26

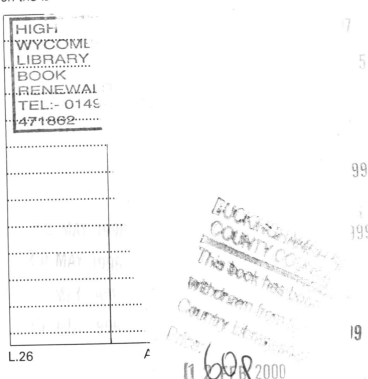

BUCKINGHAM
COUNTY CO
This Book has be
withdrawn from
County Libra

11 FEB 2000

7

5

99

199

19

Bomber's moon

It didn't sound like an everyday tragedy. Before now, tipsy yachtsmen, returning from a carouse, had blundered into the harbour and failed to emerge again. Only this was different: this was another country's national, someone special, someone unusual.

A Lübeck industrialist and once decorated Luftwaffe pilot from Hitler's war on a sentimental visit to Suffolk, where he'd been shot down on a raid and subsequently had enjoyed life among the farming folk as a POW, had been fished out of the sea – quite dead – after a late-night knees-up in the Mariners.

Superintendent George Gently, at the express behest of the German Embassy in London and Scotland Yard's Assistant Commissioner (Crime), pondered over possible motives (Political? Racial? A fight in the boozer prolonged? A family vendetta? Woman trouble?) as he considered the suspicious bruising and the blood on the fibreglass dinghy the German had moored nearby.

The wholesale suspicion of the Harford fuzz all pointed in one direction, but Gently remained unconvinced as some patient probing among the locals brought forth a remarkable story of passion and tragedy, long hidden under five decades of memory and denial.

The sedulous Superintendent once again confirms his reputation to wind up his forty-second case with a water-tight conviction in Alan Hunter's taut and page-turning new crime novel.

Other murder cases investigated
by Chief Superintendent Gently, CID.

BOMBER'S MOON

Alan Hunter

BUCKS COUNTY LIBRARY

HIW | ASK | 221661

Constable · London

First published in Great Britain 1994
by Constable & Company Limited
3 The Lanchesters
162 Fulham Palace Road, London W6 9ER
Copyright © 1994 by Alan Hunter
The right of Alan Hunter to be
identified as the author of this work
has been asserted by him in accordance
with the Copyright, Designs and Patents Act 1988
ISBN 0 09 473730 4
Set in Linotron Palatino 11pt by
CentraCet Limited, Cambridge
Printed in Great Britain by
Hartnolls Ltd, Bodmin

A CIP catalogue record for this book
is available from the British Library

The characters and events in this book are fictitious;
the locale is sketched from life.

1

'*Sprechen Sie Deutsch*, Gently?'

'Pardon, sir . . .?'

The Assistant Commissioner (Crime) wasn't usually facetious. But this morning there had been a glint in his eye as he stared across the desk at Gently.

It wasn't the brightest of mornings. Fog encompassed the city and the traffic seemed to have been denser than usual. Gently had arrived late for morning conference, in fact just as his file-bearing colleagues were leaving, and he had been ready with an excuse as the AC beckoned him to a chair.

This was the fag-end of October. Gabrielle had left for France the previous evening. As always at this time, she wished to superintend the ordering of stock for her business in Rouen, the business now run by her partner, Andrée, but on which his wife kept a firm hand. Christmas was not far off, yes? Just a few days she must spend in Rouen. So she had taken the evening flight, leaving him to return to an empty flat.

And the fog, the traffic, hadn't helped his mood. Even his morning pipe had tasted foul.

'Would you describe yourself as authoritative and discreet?'

Now the AC was quizzing him with narrowed eyes.

'I'm sorry if I'm late, sir. But the traffic – '

'Please! Just pay attention, Gently.' The AC took a swig

from a cup of black coffee. 'Now. We've had a call from the German Embassy. One of their nationals has come to grief down your way, in Suffolk. A distinguished man, apparently, the head of an electronics firm in Lübeck, and on top of that a former Luftwaffe pilot with an Iron Cross to his name. He was over here on a yachting trip with two of his family and they touched in at Harford to meet some acquaintances – a knees-up at the local pub it sounds like – and after that he went missing. Well, this morning he was taken from the river, and the locals aren't happy about it. Neither is the nephew who was sailing with him. It was he who got on to the Embassy.'

'They suspect foul play?'

'Some naughty bruising, though he may have got that tumbling in. But the locals don't like it and neither do the Embassy, who are calling for someone with the qualities aforementioned. An officer with authority and discretion. Those are the words of the Ambassador himself.'

'Could it be . . . political?'

The AC shrugged. 'If it smells, report back. But that wasn't the impression I received. They just want it firmly and quietly tidied up.' The AC referred to a report-form. 'The man's name is Gunther Herschfeldt, age seventy-three, boss of Herschfeldt Electronics. The nephew's name is Wilhelm Schmeikel. Then there's Schmeikel's wife, no name given. Schmeikel is also in the firm, probably the old man's second-in-command. And their yacht is the *Electra of Hamburg*. That appears to be all we've got.'

'Do we know who Herschfeldt was meeting at Harford?'

The AC shook his head. 'This is only just in. No doubt the locals will have the information, but what I want is you down there showing your face. Then I can give the Embassy a tinkle. And Gently, remember – authoritative and discreet.'

Grumpily, he'd gone off to his office to collect the overnight bag he kept there. Outside the fog showed no sign of lifting or the traffic of sorting itself out. The devil take gallivanting Continentals and embassies who demanded the presence of the Yard! Tonight, Gabrielle would be ringing an empty flat, and he could be sleeping in some country inn . . .

The mood lasted until he had unravelled the city and struck the familar A12, and then a red disc began to show through the murk, and the autumn foliage of trees and hedges.

By Eastwich the sun was mistily established. He arrived at Harford soon after eleven. Little excitement was apparent in the sleepy square on one side of which stood the tiny police station. He parked and went in. He found Aspall, the County CID man, closeted in the office with his henchman, Slatter. Aspall rose uncertainly to shake hands. He said:

'Good lord, I never dreamed they'd be sending you, sir!'

'Don't mind me. Just order up some coffee.'

Gently took a seat and began filling his pipe. After staring a moment, Aspall signalled to Slatter, who left to execute the errand. Then, shaking his head, Aspall resumed his seat, and watched in silence as Gently lit the pipe.

'They didn't ring you?'

'No one told us anything!'

'Was it from here that Schmeikel rang his Embassy?'

'Yes, but it was all in German . . .'

'That's the reason why I'm here.'

'The reason . . .?'

'Herschfeldt drew a bit of water. The Embassy felt he rated someone from the Yard, so the AC picked me.' Gently puffed. 'I suppose you do have a case here?'

'A case – well!'

Aspall gestured helplessly. 'As a matter of fact, I was just talking it over with Slatter!'

'Suspicious bruising – that sort of thing?'

'Well, yes. There's a gash on the head, too. But that happened when he fell in. We found blood on the stern of the dinghy he had moored there. And the bruising, that may have happened earlier – don't forget he'd spent the evening in the pub. He could have been squiffy when he got back there, caught his foot on something, and there you are.'

Gently puffed. 'I don't like the bruising.'

'But it could have happened that way, sir.'

'Any evidence that he was in a fight at the pub?'

'Well no, sir. None we've come across.'

'What does the doctor say?'

Aspall shook his head. 'Just that the bruising was recent, and sustained before death.'

Slatter returned, bearing a tray. Aspall grabbed his mug and drank greedily. Slatter retired with his to a seat at a distance. Gently took a cautious pull.

'Suppose you give me a narrative,' he said. 'Wasn't Herschfeldt in Harford to meet some friends?'

'Don't know they were friends exactly,' Aspall said. 'They were people he hadn't seen since the end of the war. Farming people. Name of Hardyment. They've got a farm a few miles up the road. Seems he ran across them at Grimchurch on Sunday, and they arranged to meet up again here last night.'

'He knew them . . . during the war?'

'That's right. Seems he was a POW. He got shot down on a raid, and later they had him to work on the farm. Then he was repatriated after VE-Day, and that was the last they saw of him till Sunday.'

'And they met at Grimchurch?'

'At the bird reserve. Herschfeldt had moored at Wolmering on Saturday. He rented a car and drove to the reserve to take some photographs there.'

'They say he was keen on birds, sir,' Slatter said. 'I had a talk with old man Hardyment. He used to be watching them back on the farm, and old Hardyment used to show him his bird books.'

'So . . . at the reserve?'

'They were in the coffee room,' Slatter said. 'Then he walked in, and stood staring at them. And they sat staring at him. Then they were shaking hands all round, and he sat down, and they had a good old yarn. Would you know the place, sir?'

Yes, Gently knew it, the white-walled building on the cliff-top, the ranging beach, curving southwards, and inland the spread of pools and reed-beds. Further south still had lately arisen the silvered dome of the new atomic power station – 'St Satan's', Gabrielle had christened it. But fortunately mists often blotted it out. Gently drank.

'So they arranged to meet again yesterday.'

'Yes, down here, sir,' Aspall said. 'It was going to be Herschfeldt's last port of call before he set off back to Hamburg. They made the trip yesterday, got in here about teatime, and gave the Hardyments a ring to let them know they'd arrived. Then, around half-seven, they met at the Mariners, and had a ding-dong there till ten. Herschfeldt saw them to their cars, and after that went down to the quay.'

'On his own?'

'On his own.'

'What about his crew?'

'They'd dined at the hotel, sir. Seems they didn't fancy boozing with the Hardyments, so they took themselves off to the Castle Arms. They'd been stand-offish from the start, Mrs Hardyment said. On Sunday, they cleared off to the souvenir shop.'

'So . . . at ten, they were still at the hotel?'

9

'Well, just leaving, sir. According to them. They'd arranged to be at the quay at ten fifteen and all row back to the yacht together. She was on a buoy out on the moorings, but we've had her fetched to the quay now.'

'And they were at the quay by ten fifteen?'

'Says they were. Or soon after.'

'But – no sign of Herschfeldt?'

'Says they found the quay deserted. They reckoned Herschfeldt was still whooping it up at the Mariners. After a bit the lady thought they should go back and dig him out, but of course, he wasn't there, and that's when they started to get worried. He couldn't have gone back to the yacht, because the dinghy was still moored at the quay. During the season he might have hitched a lift back there, but not at this end of the season.'

'So they came to us.'

'Right, sir. Bartram books them in at eleven fifteen. At first he isn't too bothered, thinks maybe Herschfeldt cleared off with the Hardyments, but then he rings them, and they tell him no, the last they saw of Herschfeldt was heading for the quay. So then Bartram calls in a couple of cars and they make a search of the area round the quay, and Bartram checks the hotel and the other pub and makes enquiries at the Mariners. For good measure, he had the yacht checked too, and put out a description to the patrols. But no dice. And already he's beginning to think of the river.'

'And the Schmeikels – they remained here?'

'In the end, Bartram sent them back to the yacht. Very upset he says they were, especially the lady. She was snivelling.'

'Bartram called off the search?'

'Around 2 a.m., sir. There wasn't much else he could do till daylight.'

Gently finished his coffee and relit his pipe. After all,

didn't it sound like an everyday tragedy? Before now tipsy yachtsmen, returning from a carouse, had blundered into the water and failed to emerge again. One difference: this was someone else's national, a man a little special, a little unusual. And . . . there had been bruising: perhaps unconnected, but perhaps not.

'So. . . when did they find him?'

'It must have been about first light, sir. A fellow called Brister, a fisherman, was down there to go out and draw his nets. He spotted the body on the slipway, the one beside the quay. It was partly submerged and he hauled it ashore. He reckoned that if the tide was going up it would have fetched it in there.'

'And was the tide going up?'

Aspall nodded. 'He'd have gone in near the top of the flood. The dinghy was moored at the corner of the quay, but the flood would have swept him round to the slipway. Brister covered the body with a tarpaulin and came to report to us. Bartram got Schmeikel out to identify it, then an ambulance took it in to Eastwich.'

'Where . . . it was examined.'

Aspall nodded again. He seized his mug and drank up.

'Tell me about the bruising.'

'Well – we don't have a written report yet, sir!'

'On the chest?'

'Yes . . . some there.'

'On the arms?'

'A few there.'

'Face?'

'Just . . . the jaw.'

'Any damage to the knuckles?'

'I . . . didn't notice, sir!'

Gently said: 'In your experience, would you say that Herschfeldt had been in a fight?'

Aspall stared at his mug. 'I suppose I'd have to say yes,

11

sir. But it didn't have to happen on the quay. And the gash on his head, that's explained. It was done when he tumbled in.'

Gently puffed. 'Have you enquired at the Mariners?'

'I asked in there, sir,' Slatter said. 'They were merry and singing songs and all that, but there wasn't any trouble. Said Herschfeldt borrowed someone's concertina and had them all doing hornpipes. There was a tray of drinks knocked over, but he insisted on paying for the damage.'

'Nothing occurred to give rise to ill-feeling.'

'No sir, quite the other way about. I talked to Myrtle – she's the landlady – and she said she wished he was coming there every night.'

'You will have spoken to Schmeikel.'

Aspall said: 'I did ask if there'd been trouble at any time on the trip. But he just stared as though he didn't understand me, and his wife shook her head and said: "*Nein, nein, nein!*"'

'So wouldn't you say that narrowed it down?'

'Always suppose they're telling the truth, sir.'

Gently puffed. 'Where are the Schmeikels now?'

'I daresay we shall find them on the yacht.'

'So.'

He rose to his feet, and after a pause, Aspall rose too.

Now the sun was strong enough to throw sharp shadows in the square, where cars were parked, and to bring out detail in the tall castle keep that was a feature of Harford. It stood in a meadow at a little distance, partly hidden by the houses, and it was at that corner of the square that one saw the brick front of the Castle Arms hotel. From the quay, perhaps half a mile? Say a walk of ten to fifteen minutes. The Schmeikels would need to have left promptly at around ten to have kept their rendezvous with Herschfeldt. Then, would they have not been passed by the Hardyments, as they drove away?

'Has anyone checked when the Schmeikels left the hotel?'

Aspall was obliged to shake his head. Slatter was deputed, and departed on the errand with small hesitation.

'Do we take a car, sir?'

'We'll walk.'

Not that Gently was unfamiliar with the village. But he wanted to view the scene afresh, to fit the events that had happened there in their setting.

From the square, a street bore away to the right, passing by the wall of a handsome flint church, dipping down then between houses and cottages, the latter set behind a broad grass verge. Further down still was a public car-park, and opposite it the homely face of the Mariners. The latter possessed no parking, so it was across the road that Herschfeldt had seen off the Hardyments. From there, the road passed an old brick warehouse, used in the season as a café and shop, but now closed, then surmounted a flood-ramp to reach a small quay that jutted out into the river. From car-park to quay, two hundred yards? And the same distance from the Mariners. But the quay lay below the flood-ramp and was otherwise obscured by the warehouse and some derelict buildings. There were no street lights, and in the capital, at all events, the previous night had been misted and overcast.

'That's her, sir. The *Electra of Hamburg*.'

A handsome ketch was moored to the quay. White enamel with gleaming varnished coamings, she had her sails smartly furled and her ropes coiled.

Downstream, a few yachts were still moored at their buoys, upstream others were shored up on the bank. There, too, were an assemblage of huts, long-shore boats and nets hung to dry.

13

'Where was the *Electra* moored last night?'

'At one of those buoys, sir. The one on the right.'

'And the dinghy?'

Aspall pointed to a bollard inboard of the downstream jut of the quay. Gently went to look. The tide appeared to be at flood slack, but there was still a drop of six or seven feet. The yacht's dinghy, a hefty fibreglass boat, trailed forlornly at the stern of the yacht.

'You are policemen, yes, and you wish to speak to me?'

A man had appeared in the well of the yacht. He stood staring up at them with steady brown eyes, a hefty fellow dressed in jeans and a sailing-jacket.

'You are Herr Schmeikel?'

'Yes, I am. But you I do not think I have met before. Are you then from London?'

'I am from London.'

'Ha. Then they know their business at the Embassy. Please step aboard.'

He moved back from the rail, and extended a steadying hand towards Gently. Behind him a woman had appeared on the cabin steps, a fine-featured blonde wearing slacks and a pullover. She smiled uncertainly as Gently landed in the well, but turned away when Aspall followed him. Schmeikel took Gently's hand.

'And who have I the honour . . .?'

Briefly, Gently gave name and rank.

'Ah yes, is good, you are very welcome. And you have come to clear up this sad business?'

'I have been seconded to the case.'

'Seconded, yes. So please be good enough to come inside.'

The woman made way, and Gently descended the steps, followed by Schmeikel and the hesitant Aspall. The steps plunged them into a spacious cabin furnished with luxurious sofa-berths, and including a bar. Schmeikel headed for the latter.

'A glass of schnapps, yes? Or whisky-scotch?'

'Not for me.'

'Then coffee, perhaps? Trudi, switch on the percolator!'

'No coffee either.'

'No?'

'I am here on business, Herr Schmeikel.'

'On business, yes, of course. But may we not be sociable too?'

'I would sooner you both sat down and gave me the information I am seeking.'

Schmeikel stared as though he didn't quite follow, but then took a seat on one of the sofas. His wife seated herself decorously beside him and folded her hands in her lap. Of the two, she seemed the more apprehensive, lacking in the ready confidence of her husband. She was the younger by several years. Schmeikel would be a man in his late forties. Full-faced, dark-haired, he had the air of one who was used to being obeyed.

Gently seated himself opposite them, across the cabin table: after a bit, Aspall squatted on the steps. Gently said:

'Now. As I understand it, you chose not to accompany your uncle last night. While he entertained his friends in the Mariners, you preferred to have dinner at the hotel. Why was that?'

'Why?' Schmeikel made a contemptuous gesture. 'My dear Herr Gently, these people are farmers, crude, beer-swilling, little better than peasants. My uncle had the misfortune to know them, he was quartered upon them when a prisoner, but that is no concern of ours. So, we prefer dinner at the hotel.'

'Yet your uncle seemed to enjoy their company.'

'Oh, my uncle! He was very special. In his young days he was a pilot in the Luftwaffe, which gave him a taste for all manner of company. When he was with princes, he was a prince. When he was with peasants, he was a peasant. But with us, not so, yes? A little more politeness is what we seek.'

'So you avoided meeting his friends.'

'I regret, yes.'

'You retired to the hotel before they arrived.'

'By seven, we were sitting with our aperitifs and deciding what food, what wine we shall order.'

'And there you remained – the whole evening?'

Schmeikel stared. 'But yes.'

'Your wife also?'

'She will tell you.'

Trudi Schmeikel faltered: 'It is so. Is true!'

'Until – 10 p.m., was it?'

Schmeikel was still staring. 'At ten we leave to meet my uncle, so that all together we row back to our yacht. Have you not been told this?'

Gently stared back. 'I wish to have your own account of your movements. You say you left the Castle Arms hotel at ten. At what time do you say you arrived at the quay?'

Schmeikel hesitated. His eyes were angry. 'I do not like this,' he said. 'Now, you begin to treat us as criminals, my wife and I. For this you were not appointed by the Embassy.'

'You prefer not to answer?' Gently said.

'Yes, any honest question I will answer!'

'Then?'

Schmeikel stared at his wife, who shrank a little, and averted her eyes.

'Perhaps, Frau Schmeikel . . .?'

'I will answer! You have no need to harass Trudi. At ten, about, we are leaving the hotel, and fifteen minutes later we arrive here.'

'At ten fifteen. About.'

'I am saying. It is then we are joining my uncle. But, when we arrive, nobody. There is only the dinghy, still moored to a post.'

16

'On your way here, would you have met anyone?'

'In the village, yes, there are people.'

'But on the road down?'

'I think, not.'

'Were you passed by any cars?'

'I think – yes. Two or three.'

'Would you have recognised any of them – say the cars of your uncle's friends?'

Schmeikel's eyes rose to the roof. 'Where before would I have seen the cars of those people? On Sunday, no, and last night I am careful to be missing when they arrive. Is it them you suspect of foul play?'

'You can give no description of the cars.'

'It is dark. They are lights and some noise that passes by. If you say they are the cars of those people, very good, and they could have pushed my uncle in the river before they left. Yes, I like that.'

'Have you any evidence to support such an allegation?'

'They are rough peasants, yes? And full of beer?'

'And that is all?'

'Perhaps you will find more.'

Gently shook his head. He looked at Trudi Schmeikel. Trudi Schmeikel sat tensely staring at the cabin table. Gently said:

'You arrived to find no one at the quay. It didn't occur to you that something might have happened to your uncle?'

'So, he is late, he is perhaps drunk. That is all we are thinking just then.'

'And you waited for him – how long?'

'It is perhaps fifteen minutes. Then Trudi is shivering, it is cold, misty, so we go to the pub to hurry him up. There, they tell us he left at ten, he and his drunken companions, and they have seen no more of him since. Is he collapsed somewhere in a drunken stupor? That is what we think next. So we look about where he might be,

17

in the little shelter by the quay, other places. But no, there is no uncle. So, perhaps he has gone off with his friends? But we do not know where, do not even precisely remember their names.' Schmeikel made the gesture of spreading his hands. 'So what shall we do, but go to your police?'

'You had noticed nothing amiss at the quay?'

'But no, what should we have noticed?'

'No sign of a struggle – the blood on the dinghy?'

Schmeikel stared, then shook his head. 'It was dark, yes? We return with the constables, and they search everywhere with lights. But the blood they do not notice. I am finding it myself, in the morning.'

'After the body was recovered.'

'Yes. In the morning we are informed of this at the yacht, by a constable. Then, as we step into the dinghy, I see the stain of blood on the stern. At once I am thinking what must have happened, and when I view the body, yes, there is a wound. In falling, he struck the back of his head on the dinghy, and so he died. Poor Uncle Gunther!'

'It – is this we are fearing.' Trudi Schmeikel faltered. 'That Uncle is drunk, and falls in. I could not sleep. All night I am thinking that out there, in the river . . .'

Gently said: 'The wound wasn't the only injury.'

Schmeikel's stare was tight: 'The rest, that is nothing!'

'The bruising is suggestive.'

'*Ach*, on yachts such things happen! I have bruises myself. The trip has been rough.'

Gently shook his head, and Trudi Schmeikel's hand had gone to her mouth. Gently said: 'I suppose you have no knowledge of any fight your uncle may have been in?'

'A fight? You are laughable! Who should he fight?'

'I am asking you.'

'And I say no! You speak of a civilised man, not a rough-neck peasant.'

'Yet the signs are there.'

'Then ask his drunken friends.'

18

'What reason would they have to treat him with violence?'

'You ask? Was he not a famous pilot, who was bombing them during the war?'

'During the war . . .?'

'Oh yes! Here, on such a raid, he was shot down. This, I hear him telling them on Sunday – at the time, they did not know it.'

Gently stared long, then shrugged.

'So, if you do not like it, an accident. That is likely, and that is best. And we can most quickly be on our way home.'

'I'm afraid not, Herr Schmeikel.'

'But, I insist! I am required back in Lübeck. The Embassy will make all the arrangements with the body. What shall possibly keep us here?'

Gently said: 'Until the enquiry is completed I must ask you to remain in Harford, and I require your assurance that you will do so. You must stay at moorings here at the quay.'

'We – must stay?'

'I'm afraid so.'

'But the Embassy promised – !'

'We shall doubtless be in touch with them.'

Now Schmeikel was staring with wrinkled brows, and his wife was also staring. But at Schmeikel.

Outside the sun was even beginning to feel warm and was fetching a sparkle from the wavelets down the moorings. A fisherman spreading his nets paused to stare at them, but he was the only sign of life on the river-front. For a while they walked back in silence, Aspall matching his stride with Gently's; then, as they drew level with the car-park, he ventured:

'So what did you make of all that, sir?'

19

Gently grunted. 'I think they're worried,' he said. 'And that goes especially for the lady.'

'You think they're holding something back?'

'I think they could be. What we don't know is how they stood with Herschfeldt.'

'Perhaps the Hardyments can give us a line, sir.'

Gently glanced at his watch. 'If they are like some other farmers I know, they should just be coming in for lunch.'

'I'll give them a ring, sir.'

'And while you're at it, ring HQ and tell them to hurry up with the PM report. It will be interesting to know just how much Herschfeldt drank last night.'

In the square they met Slatter returning from his errand to the Castle Arms. But all he could tell them was that, as far as the staff knew, the Schmeikels had left the hotel about when they said they did.

2

The PM report, it turned out, had arrived in their absence, and was awaiting them in the office. It revealed that the amount of alcohol present in the body might well have affected Herschfeldt as a driver, but otherwise was not excessive and would not seriously have impaired his general behaviour. But about the bruising the report was emphatic. It had occurred at the time of, or very shortly before, death, while the siting and nature of the injuries irresistibly suggested an attack with fists. Concussion and unconsciousness would have followed the head injury, and drowning was confirmed as the cause of death. Some small damage to the knuckles of the right hand suggested that Herschfeldt had attempted to defend himself.

So there was the picture: cheerful, mildly pickled, Herschfeldt had strolled down to the quay to await the Schmeikels, who, by their own account, would have arrived there not more than ten or fifteen minutes later. During that interval, could there credibly have been time for him to have encountered some third person, to have quarrelled with him, engaged in fisticuffs, and been struck into the river and to his doom? Well . . . perhaps. But it stretched the imagination. The time factor almost ruled it out.

'I was watching his hands, sir, when he was waving them about.'

Gently nodded: he'd been watching them too. The sort

of injuries that Herschfeldt had sustained might well have left evidence on the hands of his attacker.

'He could have been wearing gloves, sir. It was that sort of evening.'

There had been no evidence of damage to Schmeikel's solid-looking knuckles. And would it have needed quite so many blows as had apparently been struck to knock the ageing Herschfeldt into the river? What one was seeing was an opponent more equal, an opponent intent on delivering punishment, whose anger in some way had been aroused. But then . . . the time factor intervened.

'Ring the Hardyments.'

'Right you are, sir.'

For Schmeikel, what one needed was a motive.

Aspall rang, and hung up chuckling.

'Says we can have lunch with them, sir, if we like dumplings!'

Gently drove. Aspall directed him to the 'back road' that wriggled its way from Harford to Thwaite, passing several lanes that led to farms and finally bringing the river into view again. Distant below, on the other shore, lay the bird reserve of Grimchurch. Gulls flocked on a field, trees were coloured auburn, hedges crimson with berries. A couple of ground-attack aircraft arrowed in from the sea, heading for their base a few miles inland.

'The next left, sir.'

A rough, gravelled lane led off between hedges of fiery field maple. The Rover bumbled along it in third, to bring into view a house set among beech trees. White plaster and mossy pantiles, it presented a comfortable face to the world. On parking before it stood a well-worn Cavalier, a muddy Allegro and a rusting three-door Metro. As Gently parked beside them a figure appeared on the steps that led to a columned porch.

'That's Willum, sir – the old man! They tell me he's ninety-two.'

Whatever his age, Willum hopped down spryly to meet the two visitors. A short, slight figure dressed in a suit of ancient tweed, he grabbed Gently's door and lugged it open, a smile spread over his rosy features.

'You found your way then, did you?'

'We found our way,' Gently said.

'Ah, but some on them don't,' Willum said. 'That bloke with you had a job, last time. Went to Thwaite and back he did, and thas no good him saying any different. But now, you'd better come in, together. There's time for a quick one before we sit down.'

He led Gently and the pink-faced Aspall up the steps and into the house. There they were met by a dumpy-figured matron who emerged from the kitchen, wiping her hands.

'About poor old Gunther, is it? Well, I daresay it'll keep. The men'll be here in a minute, and we're just going to dish up.'

'Give us some of that Adnams, Mabs,' Willum said. 'We can't have them going dry.'

'Just you take them into the parlour, Willum,' Mabs said. 'And I'll see what I can do.'

She hastened back into the kitchen, and Willum showed them into a room across the hall. A gloomy room with gloomy, old-fashioned furniture, though with a modern TV set occupying a corner. Willum waved them to chairs and went out again. Shortly he returned bearing a tray. The beer came in a large jug, from which he deftly decanted it into mugs; then, when both had been served, he filled a smaller mug for himself. He lifted it.

'So here's to that poor old bugger, Gunther! I give him a wave when we drove off, but I never thought it'd be the last time I'd see him.'

Gently drank. The beer was cold and sweet. He said: 'You had a good evening at the Mariners?'

'Ah, we did. A real clinker. My pins was wobbly at the end of it.'

'There was music, I'm told.'

'Music, ah. Now he really *could* play a squeeze-box! He got me going along with the rest of them, and Myrtle too, her what runs the place. "Give us the Yarmouth Hornpipe" I say. "I'm buggered if I know that one," he say. So I hums it over to him, and blast me he got it, and soon he has the whole pub tapping away.'

'I believe glasses were broken.'

'That was nothn'. And Gunther, he pays for that like for everything else. It was his evening, he says, we weren't to spend a penny. Thas the sort of bloke Gunther was.'

'An evening free from trouble.'

'W'yes. What sort of trouble would there be? As soon as he got hold of that squeeze-box he had everyone falling over him. They were calling out for tunes, and he was playing them, and they were singing and kicking their toes up. And to think it ended the way it did with poor old Gunther in the river.' Willum drank. 'I waved to him,' he said. 'As we drove away, through the car back-window. And he saw me, and he waved back, standing there in the road.'

'Standing there alone?'

'W'yes.'

'No other people left the pub to see you off?'

'No, why should they? He'd bought them a last round, so I reckon they were back there lined up at the bar.'

'And Gunther – was he, too, wobbly on his pins?'

Willum drank, and shook his head. 'That want the way of it, I do know. He was always one who could hold his drink.'

'Of course . . . you had known him at an earlier period.'

24

'Ah.' Willum's blue eyes sparkled for a moment. 'Only there want much beer around in them days – the ruddy Yanks used to drink the pubs dry. But we did have a booze-up once or twice, never you mind how we got it, and Gunther drank his share with the rest. And he could always climb the steps to the loft afterwards.'

'And last night he was little the worse?'

'Saw me across to the car, didn't he?'

'At around ten o'clock.'

'Ah. We're farmers, boy, got to think of the morning.'

At which point the parlour door opened and a weather-beaten face peered round it, to announce, in a gruff voice: 'Mabs says to tell you to come to the table.'

'Right you are, Jimmy lad.' Willum said. And to the others: 'You'd better drink up! She's wonderful strict, is our Mabs, and it never does to cross her.'

In the dining-room across the hall two men were already seated at the spacious, old-fashioned mahogany table, and a narrow-featured lady wearing an apron was carry-ing steaming dishes across from a service-hatch. On the other side of the hatch a red-faced Mabs was handing up the dishes, and a savoury atmosphere of stew and greens hung heavily in the room.

'Sit you down!' Willum said. 'Don't stand on ceremony. This here is my boy Jimmy, and thas his boy Nellie. I never did get your name.'

Gently told him. The name seemed to strike them. Willum stared for a moment with narrowed eyes. He said: 'Blast, you wouldn't be that bloke from Welbourne, would you, the one they say has got a Froggie wife?'

'My wife is French and we do have a house there.'

'Ah, and come down here from Scotland Yard?'

Gently shrugged.

'Put it there, boy,' Willum said, thrusting out a gnarled

hand. 'We've heard a lot about you, boy. You come from Welbourne. You're one of us.'

'Ah, one of us,' Jimmy said. 'Do you hear that Mabs? He's that fellow from Welbourne.'

'Just serve the stew up, Jimmy,' Mabs commanded. 'While it's still hot. We can natter afterwards.'

So the stew was served, in deep-bodied plates, with hefty dumplings swimming in it, to be followed by the dumplings again, but this time swimming in golden syrup. Then there was a cheeseboard and coffee. It was simple. But very solid.

'Where's Markie?'

'Doing the hens. He'll be along, never you worry.'

Mabs, it appeared, was Mrs Jimmy, and the other lady her daughter-in-law, Cynthy.

'Smoke – go on. We're used to it.'

Willum had produced a well-blackened clay. Jimmy brought out a battered briar, the rest were content with cigarettes. So Gently lit up, which left Aspall, a non-smoker, to sit looking peaked over his beaker of coffee. Mabs puffed, and eyed Gently.

'So what's it about then? Is there something new?'

Gently said: 'Nothing new. Just that we need to learn all that we can.'

'If they got you over here it has to be something.'

'Your friend was an important man,' Gently said. 'The head of a large industrial firm, and a decorated pilot from the last war. His Embassy are naturally concerned and want the fullest possible enquiry.'

'Like if he was knocked off?'

Gently shrugged. 'Just whatever we can discover.'

Mabs puffed. 'So where do we come in?'

'I believe you were the last people to see him alive.'

For a while, silence in that odorous room, where the smell of food lingered to join that of tobacco smoke.

Willum was trying to blow rings, the others staring at the remains of the feast. Gently said:

.'Let's talk about Sunday. Did you recognise him straight away?'

'I did,' Jimmy said. 'Something clicked as soon as I set eyes on him. And Dad did too. I don't know about Mabs.'

'Perhaps you can describe what happened.'

'Ah.' Jimmy took a few puffs. 'We was over there for the birds, weren't we? Dad's always had a thing about birds, and this time of year there's fresh stuff about. So we took a trip over, and jammed around there, down to the hides and along to the mere. Then we came up to the caff and had our fourses before we drove back. And that's where he found us – wasn't it, Dad? He'd just got his tray down at the counter. He stood looking round him for a table, and then his eye lit on us.'

'Hadn't changed,' Willum piped up. 'Would have knowed him in a thousand. Same young fellow. Got some grey hair, but that was Gunther boy standing over there.'

Mabs said: 'I'd only met him a few times, I wasn't at the farm when he was here. But he said he remembered me. He remembered I'd worn my hair in plaits.'

'So that's it,' Jimmy said. 'He came over to our table, and started grabbing people's hands. And then we sat there yarning away till it was time to come back for the pigs.'

'He told us why he was there,' Mabs said. 'He'd come across in that yacht and was moored at Wolmering. They'd rented a car, him and the other two, and had come to take photographs at the reserve.'

Gently said: 'Did he introduce his nephew?'

Mabs sniffed. 'Him and her. But they cleared off into the shop, seems we weren't good enough for them.'

'Did he speak of him?'

'Said he worked for him. Said he was the son of a sister

27

who died. Said he'd be getting a slice of the business.' Mabs's eyes were sharp. 'And now it looks as though he's got it.'

Gently puffed. 'So they were on good terms.'

'No doubt he'll say they were, if you ask him.'

'Oh, go on, gal!' Jimmy said. 'You got your knife into them, and you know it. Old Gunther spoke like he was real fond of him, spite of him acting so unsociable.'

'So where were they last night?' Mabs spat.

'They didn't want to stand in old Gunther's light. We were his pals, not theirs, so they just left us all to get on with it.'

'Ha,' Mabs said. 'And ha.'

'You're giving him a wrong impression.' Jimmy said.

'Someone is,' Mabs said. And she stubbed out her cigarette and lit another.

The grandson, Nellie, also stubbed out his cigarette. He said: 'Wasn't there some talk of an anniversary – about why he was here, I mean, why he'd come over just now?'

'Ah,' Jimmy said. 'Ah, there was. What was that date he mentioned, Dad? October something in '44 – yes, of course! The 21st.'

For a while the patriarch had been staring in a dream, but now the sparkle was suddenly in his eye. He said: 'And thas a date he kept wonderful quiet about, when he came to help out here!'

'But why was that, Grandad?' Nellie said. He was a serious-faced man in his forties. Till now he and his long-faced wife had sat listening submissively to the chat of their elders.

'Why, where were your lugs, boy?' Willum said. 'Didn't he say that was the day he got shot down?'

'But why did he keep quiet about it?'

'Why? Corse he didn't want it known who'd bombed the airfield!'

'He – bombed the airfield?'

28

'Ah, didn't he. Thas the only raids we had out this way. But the RAF boys were too clever for him. When he came again, they had someone waiting upstairs. So poor old Gunther got shot down and shoved away in a prison camp. And after D-Day when they let him come here, he wasn't going to tell us he'd bombed the airfield.'

'He'd meet the RAF boys in the village,' Jimmy said. 'And the girls brought one or two back. If they'd known about that he could have been in trouble. I caught one of those devils once poaching with a Sten-gun.'

Gently said: 'Did the raids cause much damage?'

'Never heard they did,' Jimmy said. 'Blew a few holes in a runway. It was only a little plane he was flying.'

'Any casualties?'

'Didn't hear of none. Ah – I remember now! It was a Heinkel, a fighter-bomber. But the Spittys soon put paid to that.'

'No civilian casualties.'

Jimmy shook his head. 'He was right on target, I'll give him that. And the plane came down on the marshes – I got my grid out and went to have a look.'

'But – wasn't he hurt?' Nellie said.

'No, not him.'

'Jumped out with his parachute,' Willum chuckled. 'Found him stuck up a tree, they did. Had to fetch the fire-engine to get him down.'

'And', Gently said, 'the 21st was the anniversary?'

'Told us it was. I wouldn't have remembered.'

'The 21st was yesterday.'

'Ah, and that's why. Why we had our bit of a do down at Harford.'

'Any reason why it was there?'

'Course there was a reason. It was there he come down into a tree. He wanted to see the cop-shop again, where they took him.' Willum jiggled his pipe. 'But he never got the chance.'

29

There was silence at the dish-laden table. Then Mabs said: 'Cynthy, make us some more coffee!'

Jimmy said: 'And us, us'll have to be moving. There's that slurry job to do before feeding.'

Willum relit his pipe. He said: 'I don't know. I got this feeling it ain't so straightforward. Gunther wasn't pissed, and he want no fool. So why is he finishing up in the river?' He blew a blast of shag at Gently. 'Would you know something you aren't saying, boy?'

'Willum!' Mabs snapped, but Willum ignored her.

And slowly, Gently nodded.

Gently said: 'When you met at the reserve, did Herschfeldt talk to you about his trip?'

The fresh pot of coffee had arrived and been poured out into the beakers. The atmosphere was smoky, the windows steamed. Through them one saw the yard and a gaping cart-shed. Then, beyond that, a field dotted with shelters, where pigs roamed, grumbled, and occasionally squealed.

Willum drank and puffed. 'Got in at Lothing,' he said. 'Then they come down the coast to Wolmering. They was two days there. Said they'd had a fair trip. A bit more wind than they wanted, coming over.'

'Had he met anyone else he knew?'

'Not so far as he told us. They'd had a gas with some fishermen in the pub at the harbour – leastways he had. I can't answer for the others.'

'I can,' Mabs snorted. 'They'd have been at a hotel up in the town.'

'Well, there you are,' Willum said. 'It takes all sorts. You don't meet blokes like Gunther every day.'

Mabs sniffed and drank a peevish mouthful.

'Did he mention having any problems?' Gently said.

'Nothing he couldn't handle,' Willum said. 'That gal

was sea-sick coming over, and the nephew had them off course once or twice. Then they got the buoys mixed up some place, but it all come right in the end.'

'He seemed on good terms with his nephew.'

'Ah. The way he talked about him. Told us he'd made a promise to his sister that he'd always take care of young Willi. Said he'd brought him through the business, and now he was his right-hand man. And the gal, she used to be Gunther's secretary. He fared fond of her, too.'

'Fond . . .?'

'Don't get me wrong! I never meant nothing in that sort of way. Like she was family, thas all.' Willum took a couple of quick puffs.

Gently said: 'And what was your feeling about the nephew?'

'Him?' Willum took another puff. 'Don't want to say nothing against him, do I? Reckon I can leave that to gal Mabs.'

'But you formed an opinion.'

'Ah, maybe.' He gave Gently a shrewd look. 'And I reckon you have too, old partner. So perhaps we'd best just leave it there.'

'You weren't drawn to him.'

'Well there you are. And him the son of a sister of a gent like Gunther. Mind you, I only did see him that once, but I could tell. He was a different breed.'

Gently looked at Mabs, who said nothing. Then at Jimmy: Jimmy shrugged. Gently said:

'So you arranged to meet again, and at Herschfeldt's suggestion it was Harford. He sailed round, took moorings, and gave you a ring. Were you to meet him at the quay?'

'I took the call,' Mabs said. 'He rang here around five. I told him we couldn't be there before seven thirty because of the pigs and that. So he said he'd watch for us outside the Mariners. And that's where we found him.'

31

'Was there any sign of the other two?'

'No there wasn't – nor we didn't expect it! Gunther had told me on the phone we weren't going to be honoured by their company.'

'When he met you, he was alone.'

'Yes. He was waiting by the car-park entrance. He waved us in to a couple of places which he'd been keeping an eye on for us. And he told us the evening was to be on him – he even fetched tickets for us from the machine. And when we went in the pub he gave the landlady a bundle, and told her to let him know when she needed some more.'

Gently paused, and glanced at Aspall, but Aspall shook his head: Herschfeldt's wallet had been recovered intact with the body.

'And thas how he was,' Willum mused. 'He hadn't changed any in all these years. I mind me how he was when he came here, a young fellow who always pulled his weight. Ah, a handsome boy he was, ask some of the Land Girls we used to have.' He puffed on a dead pipe. 'Nor I wouldn't have blamed them, spite of Gunther being a Jerry.'

For a moment there was silence; it was broken by the distant slam of a door. Cynthy Hardyment's head jerked. She called:

'Markie! Your dinner's keeping hot on the stove.'

There followed the sound of footsteps in the kitchen, and the glimpse of a young face at the hatch. Then there was the clink of a dish and the scrape of a chair being drawn up.

'Been doing the hens,' Nellie said. 'Always keep him later, they do.'

Gently said: 'Was there any problem with Herschfeldt and the Land Girls?'

'Blast no,' Willum said. 'I shouldn't have mentioned

32

them. Just that I got thinking he hadn't changed much, still the same old good-looking boy.'

'He would be over seventy?'

'Seventy-three, he was telling us, and still as spry as Jimmy here.'

'A tallish man?'

'Ah. Well-built. And not a spare ounce on him.'

'He was grey,' Mabs said. 'But he had all his hair, and the sort of face that never seems to age. He'd been a widower for eleven years, he told us, and it surprised me he'd never remarried.'

'Still a formidable man, you'd say.'

Willum stared. 'You wouldn't want to cross him. Course, he wasn't a youngster no longer, but he could have stood up for himself, ah.'

Gently drew on a pipe that was also dead. 'Was there much other company at the pub?' he said.

'A few old fisher-boys,' Willum said. 'A couple of others. There weren't many.'

'No one he might once have known.'

'Never said there was.'

'Did he speak to anyone?'

'Ah, when we got going!'

'But – a serious conversation?'

Willum shook his head. 'There want nothing serious about last night, boy! Once Myrtle fetched out that concertina we was all going it hammer and tongs. Just you ask them.'

'We had a sing-song,' Mabs said. 'Then the tables were pushed back and people started dancing. Willum taught Gunther one of his daft old tunes and that really got them going.'

'The Yarmouth Hornpipe,' Willum chuckled. 'I told you. Nothing like that to tap your toes to.'

Gently said: 'Weren't glasses broken?'

33

'My stupid husband,' Mabs snorted. 'The girl was just bringing through a tray of drinks when Jimmy chose to do a highland fling.'

'It caused no unpleasantness?'

'A bloke got drenched and the girl had to sweep up the glass. But no, it all passed off. And Gunther got going with the squeeze-box again.'

'No other upsets?'

Mabs shook her head.

'Nothing that anyone might have taken exception to?'

'I can't think how. Gunther paid for the damage, and they must have doubled their take on the drinks.'

'Everyone was happy,' Jimmy said. 'You have to hand it to poor old Gunther. We were there to celebrate, and that's what we did, and I never knew a knees-up that went better.'

Gently paused. 'Then, at ten, you broke it up.'

'It was us broke it up,' Jimmy said. 'I reckon the rest were there till closing, but we had pigs to feed in the morning.'

'No one accompanied you when you left.'

'No.'

'There was no one about in the street or at the parking.'

'Nobody I saw. Can't speak for the others.'

Gently glanced round the table, but there were no takers. Gently said: 'So you bade your farewells, got in your cars, and left Herschfeldt standing in the road. As you drove away, up towards the village, would you have seen anyone then?'

They looked at each other, but shook their heads.

'Perhaps a man and a woman?'

'Don't think so,' Jimmy said. 'There was a cat what I nearly run over, but that's all I remember seeing.'

'Then higher up, in the square?'

'Might have been one or two around there.'

'For example, you didn't see the nephew and his wife?'

'No,' Mabs said firmly. 'And I would have remembered *them*.'

Gently sighed, said: 'Then it remains for me to thank you for your patience and an excellent dinner. And to ask you to ring the police station if anything fresh should occur to you.'

'Here, hold you hard!' Willum said. 'Do you got something in mind, we'd like to know it. We were friends of poor old Gunther, and you're as good as saying it want no accident.'

'Willum!' Mabs snapped.

'Well, so he was.'

'He's ninety-two,' Mabs said. 'You'll have to forgive him. And we're making the men late for their work. Though if there is . . . well, anything else?'

Gently rose from that hospitable table. He said: 'If there are any developments, we will keep you informed. But now we won't hold you up any longer.'

The others rose, all except Willum, who remained seated with a stubborn expression on his flushed old face. As he left the dining-room, Gently thought he heard the sound of hasty movement through in the kitchen.

'Just a minute, sir – if you will!'

Aspall was already in the car. Gently had paused to knock out his pipe in the tangle of undergrowth that once had been a flower-bed.

'Something you ought to know, sir!'

Round the corner of the house had hastened the young man whom Gently had glimpsed through the hatch. A tall young man, rejoicing in a beard, and clad in work-soiled overalls and gum-boots.

'You are . . .?'

35

'Markie, sir. Nellie's son . . . his real name is Noel! But I was at the do last night. And I saw something there I thought I should tell you.'

'You saw something?'

'It may not be much, but you were asking, and I thought . . .' He was blushing, and panting a little: a young man of not more than seventeen.

'Take your time,' Gently said kindly.

'Well sir – it's just this! The fellow behind the bar – I don't know his name – but he did seem to have it in for Gunther. He served me when I fetched some drinks. He said something nasty about having to serve a Boche. And I caught him giving Gunther dirty looks, and then he cleared out and left the other two serving.'

'A man behind the bar?'

'Yes. And I saw him lurking outside when we left. It may not mean anything at all, but you were asking, and I thought I should tell you.'

Gently said: 'You saw him outside the pub?'

The young man nodded. 'I came out last, with Gunther. And I noticed this fellow watching us, standing back, up against the wall. Then, when we'd crossed the road, I looked back, but he'd disappeared.'

Gently paused. 'Can you describe this man?'

'Well . . . I don't know! He's about fifty. Got a sharp-looking face, wears a tie and that. And he seemed to be giving a hand in the bar.'

'Did he speak with an accent?'

'He's not from round here. But he didn't sound like an educated man.'

'Perhaps . . . cockney?'

'Yes. Yes, he could be. But honestly, I wouldn't know.'

'Thank you,' Gently nodded. 'I may need to come back to you for a statement.'

'I – I wouldn't want to cause anyone trouble, sir. But you did say . . .'

Gently patted the young man's shoulder.

He was smiling as he adjusted his seat-belt and set the engine of the Rover purring. He glanced at his watch. He said: 'I wonder if the Mariners are still serving.'

'You – wouldn't know that man, sir?' Aspall ventured.

'In fact, we're quite well acquainted,' Gently said.

And Aspall was still staring as Gently let in the clutch and smoothed the Rover away.

3

'Chick Shavers, ex-con. He's married to the landlady of the Mariners. A few years ago he was mixed up in a case that involved a body found floating in a boat.'

Already the sun was sinking towards the horizon, where a bank of cloud was preparing to receive it. But, if anything, the low light increased the effect of the autumn colouring. The bronzed oaks, the coppery beeches seemed to have acquired a new intensity, and a stretch of bracken looked almost red below the gold tints of birches.

'Was that what he was done for, sir?'

Gently shook his head. 'That was for drug-running. The stuff came ashore here. Shavers would be waiting to pick it up. He used to stay at Myrtle's pub, and she apparently stood by him when he served his sentence.'

'She wasn't in it too, then?'

'No,' Gently grinned. 'Myrtle is very much the soul of propriety. Chick has had to mend his ways, and at least give the impression of being reformed. But perhaps, not quite. He keeps a little yacht here, which got him involved with a certain lady. It was she who was found adrift in her boat, and Chick's neck was left sticking out a mile.'

'But it wasn't him.'

'No.'

'Any record of violence, sir?'

Gently shrugged. 'I wouldn't put it past him.'

Aspall thought about it. He said: 'I suppose we shall

have to check it out, sir. But I still like the nephew better. Especially if he's included in the old boy's will.'

'Ye-es.' Gently pulled over to avoid a cyclist. 'The Hardyments ought to have met Schmeikel coming down from the village. He and his wife. The timing is tight, and I'm certain that Mabs wouldn't have missed them.'

'So like that, they could have been there earlier.'

'Earlier. Or it may have been later.'

'Earlier, sir. I'll bet they were waiting there when the old man arrived. They'd have wanted to make sure there was no one about, that everything was quiet around there.'

Gently drove on a few yards. 'And then?'

'Well, then the nephew set about him!'

'In front of his wife?'

'She knows something, sir. And perhaps he'd left her up the road to keep a look-out.'

Gently thought, then shook his head. 'I can't see him doing it with his wife as witness. If he were on his own he could represent it as an accident, but not if she were standing by.'

'But if she were up the road?'

'Then she was party to it, and knew what was intended.'

'And perhaps that's how it was, sir.'

But after a pause, Gently shook his head again.

Aspall brooded. They were approaching Harford. The church, the keep were visible above low-sunned trees. Aspall said:

'We have to remember this, sir. The Hardyments were the last people to see him alive.'

Gently shrugged. 'Can you suggest a motive?'

'It could have been something that happened earlier. When he was there as a POW. We only know what they tell us.'

'That was a long time ago.'

39

'But even so, sir.'

'There was no animosity showing at the Mariners!'

'It could have been a front, sir. They kept it up until they got him outside on his own. And then – well, a couple of them could have seen him to the quay. Or perhaps just one – Jimmy, egged on by his wife.'

Gently grinned – too improbable! He said: 'I think we can keep the Hardyments on hold. In the end, it may come down to some argument with a stranger, or an attempted mugging that went wrong.'

'I can't see that, sir. With the nephew in the picture.'

'What we urgently need is a witness. So we'll just call in at the station in case your men have turned something up.'

Slatter, however, had nothing fresh to offer, and they drove on down to the Mariners. Gently left the Rover on the park, and paused a moment to take in the scene anew. Sun glinted on the masts of the *Electra*, but the yacht itself was hidden by the flood-ramp. So too was the quay, and only the warehouse and a derelict building had windows that overlooked it. There was the waterfront, of course, with its fishermen's huts and hauled-out craft, but at around ten fifteen on a chill, foggy night there was small prospect of a witness in that direction. Had Herschfeldt been followed from the pub, after the cars of his friends had departed? That was certainly a credible scenario . . . and outside the pub there had been one loiterer! Gently let his eye run over the slightly unkempt building, its windows to the road, an open yard beside it. Adjoining it was a short terrace of ageing cottages. But Aspall's men had already checked those.

'Let's go.'

The pub door was still open, but there were no customers in the gloomy interior. A girl was collecting glasses on a tray and she turned abruptly on hearing the door open.

'We're closed, really – '

'Police,' Gently said.

'Oh. In that case, I'll call Mrs Shavers.'

'It was Mr Shavers we particularly wanted to talk to.'

'I'm afraid you've missed him,' the girl said. 'He's gone to the cash-and-carry in Wolmering, and I don't know when he will be back.'

'Eileen!' a voice called sharply. 'We're closed, Eileen!'

'It's the police, mum!' Eileen called back.

'What – them again?'

'They want Mr Shavers, mum.'

'Then they're going to be unlucky, aren't they?'

And a moment later Myrtle Shavers appeared behind the bar. She stared aggressively at the apologetic Aspall, and then at Gently, and her eyes widened.

'So they've got you on it,' she said. 'My, that Jerry must have carried some clout! So what's it all about now? What's Chick been up to?'

'If it's not too late,' Gently said, 'a pint of bitter?'

'Eileen!' Myrtle Shavers commanded. 'Serve these two gentlemen!'

Eileen hastened to fill glasses and Myrtle Shavers went across to the door, and bolted it. A broad-faced, heavy-bodied woman in her fifties, she carried about her an air of matronly authority. Eileen brought the glasses to a table, and Myrtle signified to them to sit. Then she took a seat across from them, and stared at Gently with determined eyes.

'So it wasn't an accident then, was it?'

Gently took a pull from his glass. He said: 'Were you present here all the evening, from when Herschfeldt arrived till when he left?'

'Was I present! Who runs this pub? If I left it to Chick we'd be in the poorhouse.'

'You – and Eileen?'

'Who else? Chick hangs around, but he doesn't do much.'

41

'And last night?'

'He was here, of course. But he was having one of his broody fits. I told him not to be such a fool, but what's the use? He's always been like that.'

'He didn't join in the fun.'

'No, not him. When the music started, he'd had enough. He slunk off into the kitchen, and never showed his face out here again.' Myrtle's eyes were suddenly sharp. 'Here, just what have they been telling you? I know that Chick is a bit of a bastard, but he's on the straight now, you can take my word for it.'

Gently drank. He said: 'Did Chick serve Herschfeldt?'

'Oh,' Myrtle said. 'That's where we are, is it? No, he didn't. He never spoke a word to him. When that lot came in, he sloped off to the snug.'

'There was no exchange of words?'

'Look,' Myrtle said. 'Why don't you say it outright? So Chick has got a thing about Jerries, always has had, isn't that what they've told you?'

'Perhaps something like that.'

'Yes,' Myrtle said. 'Yes, I can imagine. There's one or two around here who wouldn't stop at stirring up some trouble. So now you're after him?'

'Just following it up,' Gently shrugged.

'Him having done porridge,' Myrtle said. 'I wonder you didn't pull him in straight away.' She stared meanly at Gently for an instant, but then her tone softened. 'Listen,' she said. 'I know the Jerry upset him, especially when he heard what he'd done in the war. If it had been up to old Chick he would have slung the bloke and his pals out. But there's a reason for it. He was a kid in Lambeth during the time of the blitz. They hit his house, with him in the cellar, and he had to be dug out. He can't help it. He doesn't like Jerries. I mean, this bloke was a lovely man. But Chick only had to take one look at him, and he was off, cussing and swearing.'

42

Gently drank. 'Was Herschfeldt aware of it?'

'I thought I saw him give Chick a funny look once or twice. But if so he didn't let it upset him, and mostly Chick was serving in the snug. Then, like I said, when the fun began, Chick took himself off to the kitchen, and that's where I found him when we closed, with the TV going and a racing paper in his hand.'

'At what time was that?'

'Oh, eleven or after. I rooted him out to give us a hand.'

'All that time, he'd stayed in the kitchen?'

Myrtle's eyes were keen. 'Are you saying he didn't?'

Gently said: 'Would you have known?'

Myrtle stared at him, and then at his glass. She said: 'I don't know what you're on about, but he was there at nine when Eileen went to fetch some ice from the freezer. And when the Jerry wasn't playing the squeeze-box I could hear the TV going back there. Is that good enough?'

Gently shrugged.

'So he was there,' Myrtle said. 'Till closing. And if you're looking for someone to hang this business on, you'll have to look further than poor old Chick.' She paused. 'He was loaded,' she said. 'The Jerry. Have you thought about that?'

Gently nodded.

'It wasn't just a few quid. He was flashing a wallet that was bulging. He laid five twenties on the counter when he came in, and that was just a few off the top.'

'This was before customers.'

'Oh yes, he didn't hide it. And I've given them the names of those who were here.'

Gently glanced at Aspall, who nodded. 'We're making the rounds, sir. No leads yet.'

Gently said: 'I'm told glasses were smashed.'

'So what about it,' Myrtle said. 'Someone knocked a tray out of Eileen's hands. Things like that happen when you're having a knees-up.'

43

'There was no ill feeling.'

'Don't make me laugh.'

'Say among the regulars.'

'They were loving it. After he'd gone they swore they'd never had such a time, and wanted to know if he'd be back here tonight.'

'And no one left with him – except the Hardyments? Perhaps to see the Hardyments off?'

She shook her head. 'And why? Because the last thing he did was to pay for another round – to drink to his ship, he said, and to fair winds on his voyage back. Well, they were fishermen, weren't they? They wouldn't let him down over a thing like that.'

'And . . . Chick was in the kitchen.'

Her eyes sparked, but just then they heard the sound of a vehicle pulling into the yard. Myrtle's head jerked towards it, and Eileen paused in the act of wiping a glass. A door slammed. A man's voice called: 'Myrtle, they didn't have those blinking crisps in!' – and Chick Shavers strode into the bar: to pull up short when his eye fell on Gently. He went very still, staring. He said: 'Cripes, the Old Bill in person!'

'Come in,' Gently said. 'Don't be shy.'

'I think I need a drink!' Chick Shavers said.

'Look, Chiefie, I'm outside of this – whatever any sod has been telling you!'

Shavers had drawn himself a dram of scotch and tipped back at least half of it at the first pull. A rather jazzy figure in a plum jacket, blue slacks and suede shoes, he had come to stand by the table at some little distance from his formidable wife.

'I don't like Fritzes, I never have done, but I don't go around slinging them in the river. And I keep my nose clean these days, Chiefie. You only have to ask Myrtle here.'

A good-looking face marred by close-set eyes, and a wiry but well-muscled figure. And in those eyes, wasn't there fear? In the nervous jerk he gave as he drank?

'Sit down, Chick.'

'Yes, but I'm telling you!'

'You can tell me better sitting down.'

'Chiefie, I'm outside of this.'

'So sit down. And tell me about it.'

Finally, Shavers hooked out the vacant chair and sat, keeping his eyes from his wife. He took another swallow of scotch before grounding his glass on the table. He said:

'It isn't blinking fair. The Kraut didn't have to come here at all. He could have gone to the Eel's Foot or the Arms, so why did he have to pick on us?'

'Because we're the best pub around!' Myrtle said. 'Or would be, if some people pulled their weight.'

'But he didn't have to make such a meal of it – throwing his cash around and ruddy taking over!'

'You didn't like him,' Gently said.

'So why should I?'

'You decided to retire into the kitchen.'

'That's my affair!'

'You were there at nine o'clock. You were also there at eleven, or just after.'

'I was there, isn't that what matters?'

Gently stared, and shook his head.

'But I bloody was!'

'At ten o'clock?'

'The whole lousy time – I never shifted.'

Gently said: 'According to a witness, you were outside the pub when the Herschfeldt party left. Then you rapidly disappeared. The description we have fits you.'

'So some bugger's lying!'

45

'They could have no reason to lie.'

'I tell you . . .'

'Yes?'

Shavers stole a glance at the malevolent face of his wife. He said: 'All bloody right, then! I just stepped out for a breath of air. It's a free country, isn't it? And I didn't ask to run into the Kraut.'

'You stepped out into the street?'

'Well, yes. No reason to hang about in the yard. Just thought I'd see if there was anyone about there. And then out came that lot along with the Fritz.'

'You lying toad!' Myrtle exploded. 'You swore blind to me you'd never been out there.'

'It was just a breath of air, Myrtle – '

'If it was only that, why lie about it?'

Shavers grabbed his glass.

Myrtle said: 'You were up to something, weren't you? You had it in for that Jerry – and you and me know why.'

'Honest, it was nothing – '

'Don't lie to me!'

'There isn't any need – '

Myrtle's head jerked back. 'Tell them,' she said. 'Tell them. If you don't, I will. I'm not going to cover up for you, Chick Shavers. You lied to me, and now we'll have it straight.'

Shavers threw back the rest of his drink. He darted a quick look at Eileen, who was hovering agog behind the bar. Then he shrugged. 'Oh, bloody hell! It wasn't such a big deal after all. Look, Chiefie, you and me know each other. We talk the same language.'

'Chick,' Myrtle said.

'All bloody right!' Shavers said. 'I'm going to tell him, give me a chance. Yesterday I was down at the quay, wasn't I. And I saw this sodding big yacht moored to my buoy. Well, I pay dues for that buoy, and I wasn't going to have that, was I. So I unhitched my dinghy and rowed over to have a word with them.'

'We're talking of Herschfeldt's yacht,' Gently said.

'The Fritzes' boat,' Shavers said. 'I mean, there were other buoys, weren't there. No sodding reason for them to pick mine.'

'And you pointed this out to them.'

'Well, wouldn't you?'

'But they refused to move.'

'Bloody point blank. Oh he was polite about it – these Fritzes can be. Said they were tired after a rough trip. Said they'd got a meal going, and all that. Offered to pay me for the use of the buoy.'

'And did he pay you?'

Shavers' eyes were bitter. 'Pulled out that bloody fat wallet, didn't he. Peeled off a twenty and tried to hand it to me. And I just spat on the Fritz's money. So then the bugger shrugged and put it away again and frigged off down below, and the other Fritz came and glared at me, and waited till I shoved off. Oh I was raw, I don't mind telling you. But there wasn't no more to it than that.'

'No more to it.'

'No – I'm telling you.'

'And later, by pure chance, you were waiting outside the pub.'

'Look, Chiefie, I explained all that – '

'Chick,' Myrtle Shavers said. 'Stop being a lying toad.'

'Oh sod it, sod it!' Shavers groaned. 'Eileen, for Christ's sake bring me another drink!'

The drink was fetched and Shavers quaffed it thirstily, bringing a fresh flush to his unhappy face. He set the glass down before him and stared at it for several moments.

'Chick,' Myrtle Shavers said.

'All right, all right!'

'You were up to something, weren't you?' Myrtle Shavers said.

'All right, yes I was. I felt the sodding Fritz had asked for it.'

'So what little game were you on?'

Shavers took another desperate quaff. 'I went down there,' he said. 'Down to the quay. But don't get me wrong. I wasn't laying for the sod. I was back again before he came out.'

'So what were you up to?'

'Listen, will you! I was going to shift his frigging boat. I could have done it. The tide was slack. It wouldn't have taken me very long.'

'So – that was it!'

'Well, he'd asked for it!'

Myrtle Shavers gazed at her shrinking husband. She said: 'I suppose you weren't thinking of setting it adrift?'

'No I wasn't! I bloody wasn't!'

'Hold it!' Gently said. 'Let's stay with the facts. At some time after nine o'clock you left the pub and went down to the quay?'

'Yes, I'm saying – '

'Can you give an exact time?'

'Near enough it was quarter-past. But – '

'And you came back when?'

'I don't bloody know! It was just as the Fritz and his pals were leaving. I could see them on their feet, through the window, so I hung back, out of the way. The Fritz was the last to come out, and I spat after the sod, and nipped into the yard.'

'You were in the yard when the cars left?'

'No – inside.'

Gently said: 'We seem to have no confirmation of that.'

'But it's true, Chiefie, I swear it! I was never outside again after that.'

48

Gently shrugged. Shavers quaffed. Gently said: 'And your intention to interfere with the yacht was abandoned?'

'Bloody yes. They'd have told you soon enough if some sod had monkeyed with their moorings.'

'Why was that?'

'Why? Because – because some silly bastard was parked there.'

'A car was parked there?'

'Yes, I'm telling you! So I couldn't play games with him watching me. I hung about hoping he would go, but in the end I had to give up.'

'A – car you knew?'

'Why should I?'

'Just a car,' Gently said.

Shavers almost choked over his drink. 'Look, I'm telling you the truth, Chiefie. It all happened just the way I said. I went down there to do that job, but he was parked there, and I couldn't.'

Gently stared hard at the wilting Shavers. He said: 'I want the truth from you, Chick. If there really was a car parked down there, then I need to have its description.'

'But I didn't notice – '

'A description, Chick.'

Shavers shook his head helplessly. 'It was dark. I never properly saw it. It was parked over by the slipway.'

'The size?'

'It wasn't a big one. Could have been a Fiesta.'

'The colour?'

He shook his head again. 'Might have been black. Might have been blue.'

'And it had a driver sitting in it?'

'Yes, and I could see the sod watching me. He turned to look as I came over the hump and all the time I could feel his eyes on me. Of course, I kept clear of him. I stayed

49

over by the dinghies. I kept hoping to hear him go. But time was getting on, and the sod might have known me. So I gave it up and came back here.'

'He – might have known you?'

'Well, I couldn't risk it, could I?'

'You thought he looked familiar?'

'Didn't say that, did I! It was bleeding dark, he was just a face, I can't tell you any more than that.'

Gently glanced at Aspall, who looked blank. Gently said: 'I hope – for once – you are telling the truth, Chick. Because the facts are that you were adrift between nine and eleven, with every opportunity to have followed Herschfeldt to the quay, or to have been there when he arrived. Do you wish to change your story?'

'But it's the frigging truth, Chiefie! I was back here when I said. I spit after the bastard, then nipped inside, and never went out of the pub again.'

Gently look at Myrtle.

'Chick,' Myrtle said. 'You just look me in the eye, Chick Shavers.'

Desperately, Shavers jerked himself about and submitted to the gaze of his spouse.

'Now,' Myrtle said, 'you louse. Was it you?'

'Myrtle, for Christ's sake – !'

'Was it, Chick?'

'No, Myrtle. No.'

'You're sure?'

'Cross my heart, it was all like I said!'

Myrtle stared for a long time with her penetrating dark eyes. Then she gave a little shrug, and nodded towards Gently. Gently said:

'We shall need your statement, Chick. You will accompany us to the police station.'

'But Chiefie – you're not going to pinch me!'

'Just your statement, Chick. For the moment.'

'Oh . . . bloody hell!' He snatched at his glass.

'You do what you're told, Chick,' Myrtle Shavers said. 'And let it be a lesson to you, my man.'

Behind the bar, Eileen's hand had flown to her mouth.

Outside the sun had departed to leave the western sky in a fiery glow. Gently glanced again towards the quay and the twin masts, now glinting rosily. He said to Aspall:

'You take him in. And we'll need a fix on the driver of that car.'

'Do you think he exists, sir?'

Gently shrugged. 'If he does, his testimony may be vital. So put a call out, and a release for the press and local radio.'

'Right you are, sir.'

'Meanwhile, I think I'll have a chat with the Schmeikels.'

Aspall departed with the wretched Shavers. Gently continued down to the quay. Lights showed dimly in the cabin of the *Electra*, and drawing near he caught the savoury smell of frying in progress. Schmeikel must have been on the watch, because he emerged in the well as Gently approached. He made his heavy face into a smile and held out his hand to help Gently aboard.

'You have perhaps news for us, Herr Gently? Soon, now, we can be catching a tide?'

'Perhaps not quite yet, Herr Schmeikel. But our enquiries are proceeding.'

'Not yet? But you have interrogated the peasants?'

'We have spoken to the Hardyment family.'

'And they are admitting this?'

'They have described the events that took place last night at the Mariners, and after.'

'Ah yes, and after!' Schmeikel rubbed his hands. 'Herr Gently, of this we have been giving much thought. For, is it not so plain that what we have here is the simple result of just such an orgy? They are drinking, at first, oh very friendly! But then the booze begins to tell. Now they know who my uncle was, a Nazi pilot who came dropping bombs on them. He has killed Englishers, yes? He is their enemy come back again. Why should they not now take a revenge, when all is set up, and so easy?'

Gently shook his head.

'You do not like?'

'We have no evidence that such was the case.'

'*Ach* no! There will be no evidence, they are all together in one story. But this is surely what occurred. One, two of them go with my uncle to this place. They will wait with him, see him off, stay with their great friend till the last. And then, pouf! Goodbye you German, who came bombing us in the war. And they are away and in their cars before we arrive at the fatal spot.'

Gently said: 'I repeat. There is no evidence.'

'No evidence, *nein*. You cannot hang them. But shall it matter? Because, no evidence, must we be kept for ever here? You shall advise the Embassy, yes, and make your report to Scotland Yard. And then, before the autumn storms, we may set sail for home.'

Gently said: 'The enquiry is incomplete.'

'But what shall further enquiry get you?'

'Regrettably, it must continue.'

Schmeikel made noises of impatience. 'Herr Gently, do you not understand? I am not some mechanic in our industry. Especially now we have lost my poor uncle is my presence required in Lübeck. Also the autumn storms are due, and we are short of a hand in our crew. Were you not sent to expedite this matter, to overcome the delays of the rustic *polizei*?'

Gently shook his head.

'Then – then, what is the purpose of this visit, Herr Gently?'

Gently said: 'May I request your good wife's presence?'

'Trudi!' Schmeikel rapped. 'Trudi, stop what you are doing and come out here!'

There was a jerky sizzling from up forward, and the sound of a pan being shifted. Then the blonde head and anxious features of Trudi Schmeikel appeared above the steps.

'So!' Schmeikel rapped. 'What now?'

Gently said: 'Last night, when you returned to this quay. Would either of you have noticed a car, perhaps parked over there, beside the slipway?'

'A car – did the devils bring a car here?'

'Did you notice a car?' Gently said.

Trudi Schmeikel was looking fearfully at her husband. Willi Schmeikel made an impatient gesture. 'There was no car. We would certainly have seen it.'

'And – Frau Schmeikel?'

'Oh no. I didn't see one!'

Gently said: 'It may perhaps have passed you as you returned from the village.'

Why was Trudi Schmeikel staring at her husband like that?

Willi Schmeikel said: 'Yes, cars are passing us, this we have already said. But where they come from, who knows? From the park, from here, we cannot tell that.'

'But a single car – on its own?'

'Yes, then I say. There was such a car.'

'Small, and dark-coloured?'

Schmeikel threw up his hands. 'Lights, lights, it was just lights!'

'And your wife, did she see it too?'

'I – I don't really remember!' Trudi Schmeikel faltered. 'But if Willi says yes, then there was one. I am sorry, I did not notice this.'

'Can you remember where it passed you?'

'*Nein*,' Willi Schmeikel said. 'And what is all this about a car, Herr Gently? Is it in their car that the peasants drove him down here?'

'A car has been mentioned.'

Willi Schmeikel shrugged. 'Then, quite certainly, it was theirs. And, once more, they are plainly the culprits, and there is no need to keep us here longer. Is that not so?'

But Gently shook his head – did he hear a small gasp from Trudi Schmeikel? Up forward the sizzling sound had died away, and the cooking odour had cooled on the evening air.

4

Gulls were lamenting over the moorings as Gently climbed back ashore, and upstream a pair of unusual-looking geese were stemming the ebb and poking at the rushes.

That way lay Shinglebourne and Thwaite, the other way several winding miles to the sea; the sea that, though invisible from the village, was divided from the river by only a narrow belt of marsh and marram dunes.

Across there the drugs had come, fetched from Holland by a Dutch skipper, and across there Shavers had waited in his dinghy, with a suitcase of notes at the ready. So he had served his sentence, married his Myrtle, and the Dutch fishing-boat no longer touched in behind the sand dunes . . . but? For one reflective moment Gently turned to stare back at the *Electra*.

Then he shook his head. Again – too improbable! What need had Herschfeldt to meddle with the drugs trade? Furthermore Customs would have boarded the yacht when it arrived at Lothing, where it would scarcely have landed if it were carrying contraband. And yet . . . if that car had been waiting at the quay? Could Herschfeldt have stumbled on something down there? Shavers' explanation for his presence there was questionable, and he wouldn't think twice about shopping an associate. He knew the ropes, had the contacts, kept a dinghy ready at the quay.

And then, if Herschfeldt had blundered into that, it would become a case of every man for himself!

And the Schmeikels, could they be entirely dissociated? Once more, his gaze returned to the *Electra*. Why was Schmeikel so eager to be gone, and his wife in such a state of nerves? About the tragedy they exhibited little grief – the Embassy could make arrangements about the body! While any scapegoat would serve for a culprit – a stupid detail required by the rustic *polizei* . . .

A connection somewhere? Schmeikel with a drugs drop?

A face was peering at him through one of the ports.

Gently shrugged, and turned on his heel, while the wheeling gulls continued to wail.

He fetched his car and drove back to the police station. On his way he met Shavers returning to the pub. The ex-con went by with eyes firmly averted, but, in his mirror, Gently saw him turn and thumb his nose after the retreating car.

'Only one thing fresh has come in, sir. Someone rang Slatter while we were away.'

Gently found Aspall in the office, brooding over a statement in Shavers' flamboyant script. A coffee-tray stood on the desk: Gently poured himself a mug. Then he lit his pipe and sat. He ran his eye over the statement, which Aspall pushed across to him. Shavers' memory seemed to have improved: the colour of the car was now definitely blue. Also he had seen some more of the driver, who now he thought 'looked like a wrinkly'. An elderly man, in a modest car? It scarcely sounded like a link in a drugs ring. But then, to mislead them could be Shavers' intention. Gently pushed the statement back to Aspall.

'We need to trace that car – if there was one.'

Aspall nodded. 'I've already done what you suggested,

56

sir. It'll be on the next news on Radio East Anglia, and in the local paper in the morning. Then I've put a man on enquiring in the village. But we really don't have much of a description.'

'The driver could have been a witness. Or something else.'

'We still have only Shavers' word for him, sir.'

'Schmeikel may have seen the car leaving.'

Aspall shook his head, and stared at the statement. He said: 'When you think about it, sir, there's only one gainer in this business. And if Herschfeldt was who they say he was, there must be a fair old whack involved.'

Gently puffed, and then nodded. He said: 'Schmeikel wants us to think the Hardyments are to blame.'

'But that's ridiculous!'

'A drunken revenge. On the enemy who bombed them during the war.'

'But they weren't drunk, sir. And he didn't bomb them.'

'The car, if there was one, being theirs.'

Aspall shook his head decidedly. 'That's tripe, sir. It has to be. All we know about that car is that it was already parked at the quay.'

'We forget the Hardyments.'

'They never were on, sir. I'd sooner take Shavers for the job. He was there, and he had it in for the old boy. And with him there's a record to top it off.'

'Myrtle stands by him,' Gently said.

'No, sir, no,' Aspall said. 'We come back to it. There's just one winner. And somehow we have to hang it on him.'

Gently drank coffee. He said: 'We need testimony as to just when Schmeikel left the hotel. And testimony that he was at the quay at the critical time. Without that, there's no case. Schmeikel had motive but no opportunity. And even with that testimony the DPP may not look at it.'

'But – what else can we show, sir?'

57

'We would need an eyewitness.'

Aspall stared hard. 'The man in the car!'

'If he exists. Or else a confession. And I can't see Schmeikel obliging us with that.'

'Oh, the devil, sir! Begging your pardon.' Aspall flicked at the statement lying on the desk. 'And I'm as sure as I sit here that the nephew is the man we're after!'

Gently shrugged. 'So we need that car and what the driver of it can tell us. And a double check for any testimony that can put Schmeikel on the spot.'

'Yes sir. I'll surely take care of that.'

'And meanwhile, what was it that came in?'

'Oh, that.' Aspall jerked his head disgustedly. 'Just one more anonymous phone call, sir. I'd better call Slatter.'

Slatter entered: he looked apologetic. 'Don't think there's anything in it, sir!' he said. 'Some yokel rang up about half an hour ago. He wanted to know if we'd heard about Molly.'

'About who?'

'Molly, sir. I thought he was some nutter, and nearly hung up. But then he mentioned the name Hardyment, so I listened to what he had to say.'

'And what was that?'

'Just that we should ask them about Molly, sir. Nothing else. And when I asked him who he was, he hung up.'

Gently said: 'And he sounded like a yokel?'

'Yes sir. An oldish man, I would say. And I think he was ringing from a box, because I could hear a car going by.'

'A joker, sir,' Aspall grunted. 'We do get them now and then.'

'He didn't sound like a joker,' Slatter said. 'Though I don't suppose there's anything in it, sir.'

Gently blew a smoke ring. 'We're still groping,' he said. 'So perhaps we should do what the man said. You stay and look after the other angles. I'll take a trip to Grange Farm.'

'We could give them a ring, sir,' Aspall objected.

But Gently was already on his feet.

A crimson glow still remained in the sky when he parked on the weedy gravel sweep, and only a single window was lit in the shadowy front of the farmhouse. The modest breeze had died and the tall trees stood silent: from somewhere in the distance a pig was squealing, and one heard the faint clank of a pail.

Gently got out and slammed the Rover's door. It was the only signal needed: almost at once, old Willum appeared from the back of the house and came hobbling and grinning to meet him.

'So you're here again, old partner – and in time for tea, I shouldn't wonder!'

'Are the people about?' Gently asked.

'Ah, the womenfolk are, and Jimmy. Nellie's still feeding the pigs, and Markie, he'll be collecting eggs. You wanted a word with them?'

'If it is convenient.'

'Come you in,' Willum said. 'You're always welcome here, boy. And if there's anything we can do for you, you just have to ask.'

He led Gently in. They found the two women and James Hardyment seated round a tea-tray in the dining-room. Jimmy had a newspaper in his hand, Cynthy a paperback novel. Mabs was knitting what appeared to be a sock, and was counting the stitches as her needles flew. But these activities ceased as Willum and Gently entered the room. Jimmy lowered his paper, Cynthy her novel, and Mabs, after a moment, sheathed her needles.

'Wants a word!' Willum chuckled. 'I knew he'd be back here.'

'Cynthy,' Mabs said. 'Is that tea still hot?'

Cynthy felt the teapot. 'It'll do.'

'Sugar?' Mabs said.

Gently shook his head.

'Take a seat – do!'

Gently took a seat. Cynthy poured him a cup. Jimmy folded his paper and put it down beside him. He stared a little from beneath his gnarled brows. He said:

'Got some news, then?'

'Not exactly news.'

'But something's come up?'

Gently nodded.

'That nephew, is it?'

'We have spoken to the nephew.'

'Ah,' Jimmy said. 'Spect so. We've been thinking about him.'

'A bad lot,' Mabs said. 'Real nasty. I wouldn't want him where I couldn't see him. Are you pulling him in?'

'Do you stop asking questions!' Willum piped up. 'Let the man drink his tea before you set on him, together.'

Gently took his tea and drank; the tea was both hot and strong. He put his cup aside. He said:

'If we could talk about last night?'

'Ah, last night,' Jimmy said. 'We've been having that over and over. Markie was telling us about the bloke he saw, and how sharp he was to slip away.' He paused. 'Are you on to him?'

Gently said: 'Were any of you at the quay last night?'

'At the quay . . . No, we wasn't! Never had no cause to go down there.'

'You didn't at any time drive down there?'

'W'blast, no. Is there some bugger said we did?'

'We have a report of a car being parked there.'

'Well, it couldn't have been us, old partner.'

'We parked in the car-park,' Mabs said. 'Gunther was waiting for us there. And afterwards we drove straight back home. If that fellow was about he would have seen us.'

Gently said: 'A small blue car. The driver may have been getting on in years. Perhaps you saw such a car when you were there. It would help us if we could identify it.'

Mabs looked at Jimmy. Jimmy looked at Mabs. 'I was driving the Allegro,' Jimmy said. 'That'd fit. But it wasn't me. Not if that car was seen down at the quay.'

'And you remember no other car of that description?'

'Blast, we weren't there to study cars,' Willum said. 'Now were we? Just to get across there into that pub, and get afoul of our pints.'

'And you?' Gently said to Cynthy.

Cynthy began to shake her head. Then she said: 'There was a car like that. One of the new Corsas. That's why I noticed it. But I didn't pay any attention to the driver.'

'A car on the park?'

'Oh no. It was driving ahead of us when we got there. Then it turned right, into the square. And it was blue, a blue metallic.'

'Would you have noticed the date letter?'

'Yes. An L. But don't ask me for the rest. I only noticed it at all because we fancy a new Corsa.'

'But, the driver . . .?'

She shook her head. 'I can't tell you anything about him.'

Jimmy was frowning. 'You reckon?' he said.

'Just that it may help us,' Gently said.

'He wasn't the bloke, now?'

'Jimmy, you shut up!' Mabs said. 'And Cynthy, pour him another cup of tea while it's still worth having.'

A rather warm-faced Cynthy complied, and Gently took a sip from his fresh cup. Jimmy was still frowning, and Willum had got out his old clay pipe. Between puffs he said:

'It's a rum old business, can't think who'd want to do that to a bloke like Gunther. Start to finish, he was a good'un. And you can't say that of many.'

'Of course, if we'd known at the time,' Jimmy frowned.

'He couldn't help being a Jerry, Jimmy boy. Just doing his bit, thas all it was. Like me in the '14–'18.'

'He bombed the airfield.'

'Ah. That was his job. Thas no good blaming him for doing that.'

Jimmy chucked his head. Gently said:

'One other thing I have to ask you. We don't usually pay much attention to anonymous phone calls, but one was received that referred us to you.'

Mabs' eyes were sharp. 'An anonymous phone call?'

'The caller appeared to be an elderly countryman.'

'You mean he was a yokel?'

Gently shrugged. Mabs and Jimmy exchanged looks. 'That bastard!' the latter muttered. 'Just let him wait. And what's he been saying about us?'

'You think he is known to you?'

'Damn certain he is. There's only one bloke who'd carry on like that.'

'Bert Moulton,' Mabs said. 'Jimmy sacked him. Caught him flogging eggs on the side. So what's he been saying?'

Gently said: 'He told us to ask you about Molly.'

And there was silence in the heavy room. Even Willum's pipe had stopped wheezing.

'Perhaps – shall I make another pot?'

It was the nervous Cynthy who broke the silence. She jumped to her feet and grabbed the pot: but Mabs waved her back to her seat again. Jimmy sat staring and clenching his fists. Willum's pipe had gone out. His blue eyes were misty, distant, his bony hands lying limp. The pipe shifted in his mouth. He felt for it. He quavered:

'She was a pretty gal, she was. Molly.'

'I'll break that evil bastard's neck!'

'Hush, Jimmy!' Mabs said quickly. 'We don't want trouble.'

'But going to the bloody police like that!'

'If he hadn't done it, someone else might.'

'But it had to be him!'

'Hush,' Mabs said. 'Hush. We can talk about that later.'

Jimmy's fists clenched and clenched. His malevolent stare was fixed on the table. Gently said:

'May I ask who she was?'

Mabs said tightly: 'Jimmy's sister.'

'His sister?'

Mabs nodded. 'She was older than him by a couple of years. A student teacher. During the war. She cycled into Shinglebourne every day. Big ambitions and all that. She was going to be quite someone.'

'An attractive girl?'

Mabs pouted. 'I daresay some would have called her that.'

'She was bloody lovely!' Jimmy snarled. 'You know she was, Mabs. You're just jealous.'

'And why should I be jealous?'

'You just were. She'd got all the blokes running after her. Yanks and all, though she wouldn't look at them. No one was good enough for our Molly.'

Mabs stared at him but said nothing.

'Like Jessie Matthews she was,' Jimmy said. 'Same face. Same little curl. She could have been a star up there too.'

Mabs snorted.

Willum's lips were trembling. 'Allus a smile she had,' he said. 'A smile for her old dad. Ah. She was a rare pretty gal, Molly.'

'Dad, don't you take on!' Jimmy said.

'I mind me of her last birthday. Got that new bike for her she wanted. Never rode it. Thas still around.'

'Dad!'

'I can't help it.' His cheeks were wet. 'She was your mother over again.'

Cynthy was crying silently too. She plucked a handkerchief from her sleeve and dabbed her eyes. Jimmy's eyes were ferocious. Mabs' lips were buttoned tight. Gently said:

'What became of her?'

Mabs stared at nothing. 'Took an overdose,' she said.

'An overdose?'

'Yes. She was three months gone.'

'She was pregnant.'

'Yes.'

'We', Jimmy said, 'found her in the loft room, over the barn. Where he slept. Where Gunther slept. Two days after he left to go home.'

'And – that's the connection?'

Jimmy's fists hit the table. 'Yes,' he said. 'That's the bloody connection.'

Mabs said quickly: 'Of course we don't know for certain. There were plenty of other blokes hanging round Molly. And she never left a note, nothing like that. She may only have gone there to be on her own.'

'It', Jimmy said, 'was him. It had to be him.'

'But no one ever saw her with him, Jimmy. And she was always out with the others, going to dances and that sort of thing.'

'She fancied him. I know.'

'Well I fancied him,' Mabs said. 'Oh yes – you may not think so! And me only a girl of fifteen at the time. But yes, I fancied him. And if he'd wanted me, there's no knowing what I wouldn't have done. But I didn't. And likely she didn't – her with so many blokes to choose from.'

'We found her on his bed.'

'That needn't mean a thing.'

'It was just two days after he left.'

'So then she went up there to do it, where she knew she'd be on her own.'

But Jimmy shook his head.

'Yes,' Mabs insisted. 'I'll say it again, we can never be sure. There were all those do's at the end of the war, and she was often out half the night. She was out with airmen, out with Yanks, and I saw her kissing one or two myself. And you'd have thought old Gunther would have asked after her, suppose there'd ever been anything between them.'

Gently said: 'He didn't ask after her?'

'Not a word,' Mabs said. 'May have been a guilty conscience of course. But that's not the way I'm seeing it.'

'Did she have any special boyfriend?'

Mabs looked at Jimmy. 'Wasn't there that airman?'

'It couldn't have been him,' Jimmy snapped. 'He was posted abroad a long time before.'

'Well, there were others. What about that captain, him who came around in his MG?'

'He was in the landings. Got blown up.'

'Well, I'm sure there were others,' Mabs said.

Jimmy looked very straight at Gently. He said: 'There was never any doubt with us. Not with us nor anyone else. It's always been put down to the Jerry.' He looked down at his fists. 'Isn't that the idea? Why you got that call from Moulton? That we strung the Jerry along, and then gave him what was coming to him because of Molly?'

'Jimmy, just don't talk about Gunther like that!' Willum had heaved himself up from his chair. He stood gazing down at his son, still with tears wet on his cheeks. 'You hear me, boy? I'm not having it. Old Gunther was as good as you or me. So Molly led him on, and he wasn't fireproof. But she was to blame just as much as him.'

'She was my sister!'

'Ah, and my little gal. And there was a war on. And

these things happened. And he was a long way from home and his friends, and never knew what he'd find do he ever got back there.'

'But she killed herself. Because of him!'

'Boy, thas a long, long time ago. And he never knew. And I want going to tell him. And I'm glad he never knew in the end.' He turned to Gently. 'You forget it, boy,' he said. 'There isn't nothing in what Moulton told you. We was happy as larks to see Gunther again, and a right old time we had with him. And if ever he did wrong, thas all over now. And I reckon my little gal Molly has forgiven him.'

'I forgive him!' Cynthy sobbed. 'He was lovely.'

'Gal, stop that noise,' Willum said. 'The man doesn't want to hear you carrying on. Go and make us another pot of tea.'

'But it's so sad!'

'Gal,' Willum said. And Cynthy got up and ran into the kitchen.

Gently said: 'Then it was generally believed that Herschfeldt was to blame for what happened to your daughter?'

'Ah, people,' Willum said. 'They wanted to think it. He was a Jerry.'

'There might be those not so pleased to see him back here?'

'Always,' Willum said. 'A few.'

'Could you name them?'

Willum shook his head. 'Can't rightly point any fingers,' he said. 'Old'uns like me they'd have to be, and the best part of them are underground.'

'How about the informant, Moulton?'

'He'd have just heard the tale. He wasn't around here in '45.'

Mabs said grimly: 'It's a load of old squit. There's no one in these parts who'd want to hurt Gunther. Molly

66

never did have a steady boyfriend, not one who'd bear a grudge for all this time.'

Gently said: 'You mentioned servicemen.'

'Yes. And you know what they're like! They were here today and gone tomorrow – our boys, Yanks, they were all the same.'

'But some would be local?'

Mabs thought, but shook her head. 'There was none of them stationed round here. Molly invited one or two back, but they were all boys from away. There was a Scottie, I remember him. And a kid from down London way. But none of them steadies. They just came and went.'

'Perhaps a local farm-lad?'

'Fat chance,' Mabs said. 'Molly never wasted her charms on them. And most of them were called up anyway, it was all Land Girls. I was one myself.' She sniffed. 'So it's squit,' she said. 'We know well enough who did it. And so do you. It was a bloke with a reason, and who saw his chance and took it.'

Gently drank a little cold tea.

'And it bloody wasn't us,' Jimmy added.

'Jimmy, you lay off!' Willum said. He squinted at Gently. 'You want to see,' he said. 'You want to see where old Gunther bunked down? Blast, it can't have changed much in all this time.'

'Willum!' Mabs snapped.

Willum touched his eye. 'Was going to have another look at it myself,' he said.

But the ladder almost beat him. He'd led Gently through the kitchen, across a paved yard and into a thatched barn filled with straw-bales. There, in a corner, a cobwebbed step-ladder rose to a dusty-looking trap door. Willum hobbled across to it and stood staring. Gently said:

'Had I better go first?'

Willum shook his head firmly. 'Do I can't get up there, thas time they carted me off to the graveyard!'

One step at a time, he hauled himself up, pausing after each to draw breath. Half-way up he hung on for what seemed an age before continuing the ascent. Finally, panting heavily, he reached the trap door, and there stuck again for a while. But at last, with a tremendous effort, he heaved the trap door aside and crawled into the loft. Gently followed him, gave him a hand up. A little light penetrated through a small cobwebbed window. Dimly one could see the dusty plank floor, a rusting iron bedstead, a packing case. On a hook hung a rusty hurricane lamp. Gently shook it, then, with difficulty, raised the glass and lit it. Now one could see rotting mattressbiscuits piled on the bedstead, and, peeling from the wall, a magazine illustration. Willum clung to Gently, still gasping.

'Not much of a dug-out for a bloke, is it?'

'It was perhaps different then.'

'Ah, it was. Kept it clean and tidy, old Gunther did.' Willum released Gently's arm, took a step closer to the bedstead. He lifted one of the biscuits: the rotten canvas stuck, and ripped. He let it fall again. 'Give him some good blankets, we did. And a Valor stove when it was sharp. And books and magazines I lent him, bird books. He liked them best.'

'Was there anything special at the reserve on Sunday?'

'Blast, yes! Didn't I say? Got this egret there, hadn't they. Couldn't move for blokes with cameras.'

'Enthusiasts from a distance.'

'Ah. They come from all over for a bird like that. I never did see one before, and I've been around here as long as most.'

'Did Gunther photograph it?'

'Reckon he might have. But we had other things to talk about.'

'Would he have mentioned meeting with other enthusiasts?'

'No, I tell you. We weren't talking about birds.'

He ran his hand over the packing case, which still stood by the bedstead to serve as bedside table. On it stood a rusty tobacco tin which might have been used as an ashtray. There was nothing else in the forlorn place. The magazine illustration was an advertisement for cider and depicted a scantily dressed girl with a glass in her hand.

'Found her here,' William said. 'Me.' He stroked the packing case again. 'There was a glass here. And the bottle. But your blokes took them away. Curled up like a little cat she was. Got on a new dress we'd just bought her.' He turned away. 'I've lived too bloody long.'

'Let's go down,' Gently said.

'First time,' Willum said. 'First time I've been back here. And I reckon it's the last.'

'I'm sorry,' Gently said. 'Sorry it came up.'

'Want your fault, boy,' Willum said.

Nellie and his bearded son had returned when they went back to the house, but Gently wasted no time in bidding his adieus. Mabs and Jimmy saw him off. At the junction of the lane with the road, he paused to look back. A little fiery glow still lingered in the sky, and against it the house and its trees showed black. As he watched, the single lit window went blank. Gently shrugged and gunned the Rover's engine.

He drove back to Harford slowly, thoughtfully. Still, they were groping for a lead. The cards were stacking against Schmeikel, but as yet no alternative could be ruled out. At the edge of the picture, Shavers, and beyond him an open field: a field that might stretch further than Suffolk, and extend even across the sea. Herschfeldt had been an important person but of his background they had only an outline. Had his Embassy been perhaps a little too eager to associate Scotland Yard with the enquiry?

At the police station he was met by an excited Sergeant Bartram.

'Sir, they've just had a ring – a ring from the man you want!'

'The man . . .?'

'Him who was parked at the quay, sir. He heard it on the radio, and rang in.'

Gently hastened into the office. A triumphant Aspall had just hung up. He said:

'So that's it, sir. A man called Stratton. He lives at Wolmering. And he's on his way here.'

'From Wolmering?'

'Right, sir. And he says he drives a dark blue Corsa.'

'A dark blue Corsa . . .!' Gently pulled up a chair. 'So Shavers was telling the truth. Or some of it.'

'Looks like it, sir,' Aspall said.

Slowly, Gently drew out his pipe.

5

The Castle Arms Hotel was persuaded to send across a pack of sandwiches, and while they ate them Gently related to Aspall and Slatter the results of his second visit to Grange Farm.

In the square outside, after the sunny day, mist was again beginning to form, blurring lights in the windows of houses opposite, half concealing a moon that hovered over their roofs. Passers-by were few, and didn't linger, hunched a little as they went past. The engine of a car being started sounded throaty and its lights looked pale as it drove away.

'Well, I don't know, sir.' Aspall had been staring out at the scene as he listened. 'That may have happened all that time ago, but some of them round here have long memories. And I wouldn't put it past that Jimmy character to have had a go if he saw the chance – he may be in his sixties, but he's a tough one. And like he said, she was his sister.'

'Perhaps he just meant to rough him up, sir,' Slatter put in. 'Then saw what he'd done, and panicked.'

'The opportunity was there, sir,' Aspall said. 'And they had been drinking. Drink can do things to people. It may all have started out right enough and then turned nasty. It's happened before.'

Gently grinned at them. 'Now you're talking like Schmeikel! But I think the Hardyments can hold their

71

beer. And I doubt if Jimmy would have had an opportunity without the others knowing about it.'

'They'd stand together, sir. Folk like that.'

Gently shook his head. 'Perhaps Mabs and Jimmy. Not the others. Not Willum. Not Nellie and his wife and their earnest young son.'

'They could have worked it somehow. Him and her.'

'They could never have concealed it from the family. And the timing is too tight. They would have run foul of the Schmeikels.'

'But . . . if the Jerries were later than they said?'

Gently's head was shaking again. 'Though what we don't know is if the winsome Molly had other admirers in the neighbourhood.'

Aspall thought about it. 'I don't know,' he said. 'Perhaps fifty years is a long time.'

'I wasn't born, sir!' Slatter put in.

'And yet, if the folk round here have long memories?'

Aspall thought about it some more. Then he, too, shook his head. 'Has to be an outsider, sir,' he said. 'And if we don't like the Hardyments, then the money is on Schmeikel. And perhaps this Stratton fellow can give us a break.'

'Yes . . . Schmeikel.'

'We're working on it, sir. Though we haven't come up with a clincher yet. But it must come, I've got this feeling. It's a funny old business altogether.'

'They're rum people, sir,' Slatter said.

Gently sighed. Then nodded.

'I've heard you spoken of by Andrew Reymerston, Superintendent. He is a customer at the bank. Recently he was commissioned to paint some bird pictures, and I was able to direct him to suitable venues.'

The chubby, well-polished blue car had slunk on to the

72

parking almost apologetically, and they had seen a tall, lean figure climb painfully out and pause a moment to look about him before locking the car door. Now he stood before them, an elderly man with lined, tired features and sleek white hair, dressed in a tidy zip-fronted parka, sandy trousers and trainers.

Gently said: 'You work at a bank, Mr Stratton?'

'Well – no longer!' He attempted a nervous smile. 'But yes, that has been my vocation, from which I retired some years ago. Now, I suppose, you would call me a bird man. I am honorary treasurer of the local society. It is because of the birds I was here yesterday – this is high season for people like myself.'

'Take a seat, Mr Stratton.'

'Thank you. As I told your colleague, I heard the news on the radio. At once I realised it was myself who was referred to, and I have wasted no time in presenting myself here.'

'Thank you, Mr Stratton. But please be seated.'

'And now I have the pleasure of making your acquaintance. I . . .'

Gently signalled to Slatter, who pushed up a chair, and after a short hesitation, Stratton sat. Nervous he certainly was. He jerked off the gloves he was wearing and faced Gently with appealing grey eyes. Gently said:

'So it was the birds that brought you here from Wolmering.'

'Yes.' Stratton nodded positively. 'We have a special number to ring, you know? It advised me of bar-tailed godwits on the Thwaite marshes, and I drove over and spent the day there. I'm afraid it was wasted. I didn't see them. Just the usual waders, oyster-catchers, shelduck. A raptor I saw may have been a hen harrier, but I wouldn't care to be positive about that. Are you a bird-watcher?'

Gently said: 'And then, from Thwaite, you proceeded to Harford?'

73

Stratton went on nodding. 'Yes. Yes. I'd only had a picnic lunch, you understand. So I thought I'd treat myself to a good dinner, and I knew they did you well at the Arms here.'

'You dined at the Arms – the Castle Arms?'

'Yes.' Stratton looked alarmed. 'Is there some reason . . .?'

Gently shook his head. 'No reason, Mr Stratton! But it may be you remember some of your fellow guests there?'

'My fellow guests . . . oh.' The grey eyes fluttered and looked down at the gloves. 'I think I understand now. The man was German – wasn't he? The man who was taken from the river?' Gently said nothing. Stratton jiffled the gloves. He said: 'I think the couple at the next table were Germans. Of course, they may have been Dutch, but I took them for Germans. Was that what you wanted to know?'

Gently said: 'Could you describe them?'

'Well – I'll try! He was a man of about fifty – fleshy face, heavy build, dressed in a smart light grey suit. Would that be him?'

Gently nodded. 'And the woman?'

'She was smart too – a tailored two-piece suit, ruffled blouse, a lizard-skin bag.' His mouth twitched. 'When you've been in a bank you tend to notice these things. If I'd had them in for a loan, I think we may have done business.'

'What colour was her hair?'

'She was a blonde. He was dark, almost black.'

'And they conversed in what you took to be German?'

'Yes. I'm almost certain it was.'

Gently said: 'Would you have noticed their demeanour?'

'Their demeanour . . .?'

'Whether they seemed carefree. Or perhaps less than that.'

74

Stratton considered the question with puckered eyes. 'Less, I think I would have to say,' he said. 'At times they seemed to be having a discussion, and the man seemed less than pleased. I think he kept trying to shut the woman up. But it was all in German, so I couldn't be certain.' Suddenly, his hand went to his mouth.

'Something else you remember?' Gently said.

Stratton nodded. He twisted the gloves. He blurted: 'I don't know if I should mention this – it probably means nothing at all!'

'Something about this couple?'

'About the man.'

Gently stared, but said nothing.

'I saw him again,' Stratton said. 'As I was driving away from the quay, later. I recognised the grey suit. He was coming down the road towards the quay.'

'The man – and the woman?'

'He was alone,' Stratton said.

'He was alone.'

Stratton was trembling. 'Might I have a glass of water?' he said. 'I hadn't realised, it may mean nothing. On – on the news they didn't say when this horrible thing happened.'

Gently nodded to Slatter, who departed, to return quickly with a mug of water. Stratton gulped some nervously. He kept the mug in his hand. Staring at nothing, he said:

'It didn't . . . have to be him, did it?'

Gently said: 'Let's try to take these events in order! At what time would you have left the hotel?'

'You haven't . . . arrested him?'

'Please, Mr Stratton! You drove down to the quay. Why was that?'

'Why . . . ?' He gulped water. 'I thought I explained. It's the autumn migration. Geese, waders. They touch down here. It's the first place they come to after the crossing.'

75

'But at night would you see them?'

'You don't have to! They are calling to each other all the time. That way you can identify them, even estimate numbers. I thought I would finish up with an hour down there.'

'So . . . you left the hotel at around 9 p.m.?'

'Yes. It was about then.'

'The couple were still at their table?'

'In the lounge . . . I think. Yes, he asked them to serve coffee in the lounge.'

'Did you have yours there?'

Stratton shook his head. 'I had mine at my table. I was keen to get away, to see what was happening down below.'

'Carry on.'

'Well, I collected my car and drove on down. It was misty, but there was a moon, and there was a chance of seeing the flocks come in. I parked where they said, by the slipway at the side of the quay, facing the marshes and the sea. Then I dropped my window a little so I could hear them when they came over.'

'You would have passed the Mariners.'

'Yes.' Stratton gulped water. 'They were making a noise in there, and I hoped it wouldn't interfere with the birds.'

'And did it?'

'I don't think so. A flock of Canadas dropped down at the moorings. And I heard some Brents go over, and a curlew, and what may have been greenshank.'

Gently said: 'But – apart from the birds?'

Stratton hugged his mug. 'A man. I don't know who he was. He suddenly appeared there. Over on the quay. I didn't even hear him come.'

'Can you give a description?'

Stratton shook his head. 'It wasn't the man I'd seen at the hotel. This one was slimmer, not so tall. I suppose it wasn't . . .?'

'At what time was this?'

'Soon after I parked there.'

'How long did he stay?'

'About . . . twenty minutes. At first he just stood there, over by the dinghy moorings, then he seemed to get impatient and began walking up and down.'

'He didn't come close to you.'

'No. But he kept looking in my direction.' Stratton hesitated. 'Is he the one who told you he'd seen me there?'

Gently said: 'In which direction did he leave?'

'I – I don't remember seeing him go. I could hear the Brents, and I was straining to see them. Then, the next time I looked, he'd gone.'

'And you saw no more of him?'

'No!'

'Perhaps . . . as you were driving away?'

'Does . . . does he say so?'

Gently shrugged. 'So you were alone at the quay again! Let's hear how it goes from there.'

Stratton looked half-offended, half-apprehensive. He took another pull of water. He said: 'After the Brents I heard the curlew, and then some oyster-catchers being noisy. Then it was quiet, and I was getting cold, and the mist was getting thicker. I looked at my watch. It had gone ten. I decided to give it another few minutes. So I was just about to leave when this other man came along.'

Gently said: 'You can be certain it wasn't the same man?'

'No!' Stratton wrestled with the mug.

'Though . . . the mist had thickened?'

'I – I could see him well enough. He was only a few yards away. He was taller, perhaps as tall as me, and he was humming some sort of tune. I don't think he noticed me. He just strolled across to the dinghy moorings, then stood there looking back towards the village.'

'And no other person around.'

'No.'

'Carry on,' Gently said.

Stratton's grey eyes were fluttering and he was having to stop his lips from trembling. He faltered: 'Was it – him?'

'Just tell us what happened,' Gently said.

'Yes . . . but!' He pulled himself together, helped by another swig from the mug. 'He – after a bit, he sat down on a bollard, still humming this tune to himself. Obviously he was waiting for someone. I decided there was no point my hanging on longer.'

'And that was the last you saw of him.'

Stratton nodded.

'Can you give me a time?'

'About . . . a quarter past ten.'

'And you left him alone there.'

'Oh lord!' Stratton said. 'Do you think, if I'd hung on a bit longer . . .?'

Gently shook his head. 'So you drove towards the village.'

'Yes. I remember thinking they'd quietened down when I passed the Mariners. And it was only a few yards further on that I met the man I'd seen at the hotel.'

Gently said: 'Alone.'

'Yes – alone!'

Gently said: 'We have to be quite certain of that. You can be positive that the woman wasn't with him?'

'Yes. He was the only person I met driving up there.'

'And his identity. You're positive of that?'

'I saw him quite plainly in my headlights. That grey suit and the dark hair. I can't say more. It was him.'

Gently said to Aspall: 'Who was on duty here when the Schmeikels reported Herschfeldt missing?'

'Bartram, sir,' Aspall said. 'Slatter, you have a word with him.'

Slatter went out. Stratton gulped more water. 'All this

78

has been a terrible shock,' he said. 'I little thought when I came here that I'd been so close to what happened. Will I – shall I be needed in court?'

Gently shrugged. 'The enquiry is continuing.'

Stratton stared at him unhappily, his creased face pale. 'I wouldn't want to do that,' he said. 'It must be horrible, giving evidence against someone accused of murder. But I suppose one has to, if there's a strong case. And I'm sure you won't go ahead unless there is.'

Gently shrugged again. Moments later, Slatter returned. He nodded to Gently.

'Absolutely right, sir! Bartram particularly remembered that suit.'

Stratton was reaching for his gloves. 'Then can I go now? You've finished with me?'

'Not quite yet, Mr Stratton. We shall require your written statement.'

'But perhaps . . . tomorrow?'

'I'm afraid we shall require that statement tonight.'

Reluctantly, an angular figure, Stratton followed Slatter out of the office. He forgot the gloves, and had to return for them, giving Gently an awkward little apologetic nod. When the door closed Aspall rubbed his hands gleefully.

'Shall I send a car to pick them up now, sir?'

'Not just yet.'

'But if Stratton got a look at them . . .'

Smilingly, Gently shook his head. 'We play this one by the book. We aren't dealing with a petty criminal. So we'll wait till Stratton is off the premises.'

'Well . . . if you say so, sir.'

'And ask Bartram to rustle up some more coffee.'

It was almost an hour later when a patrol car drew up outside and Schmeikel climbed stiffly out, followed by his hesitant wife. He paused to stare for a moment at the

79

police station. Tonight he was clad in a suit of maroon corduroy. His wife was wearing slacks and a thick cardigan. She sought to cling to his arm, but Schmeikel shook her off.

They were shepherded in, and Schmeikel confronted Gently.

'You have news then, that you are sending for us?'

'Please sit down, Herr Schmeikel.'

'But you are telling me? You have arrested the farmers?'

'There have been no arrests.'

'No arrests?' His eyes smouldered at Gently. 'But this is outrageous, I say! To be wasting time is not why you were sent here, and each tide that is lost may be placing us in jeopardy. Why no arrests?'

'The enquiry is still in progress.'

'The enquiry – *ach*, the enquiry! In this case, why have your men disturbed us? What can be the reason for summoning us here?'

'As I said, the enquiry is still in progress.'

'And I say, what is that to us? All we can tell you has been told, and yet this progress is leading nowhere.'

'Please sit, Herr Schmeikel. And your lady wife.'

'I demand to know your reasons!'

'We wish you to go through your movements again. Your movements of last night.'

'But – these have been told!'

'There were, perhaps, small variations.'

The brown eyes blasted his. 'Are you saying we are liars?'

'We wish merely to go over your statement again. In case some detail of importance has been missed.'

'And that is not the same, ha?'

Gently motioned to a chair. After glaring a little longer, Schmeikel dumped himself on it. All this while Trudi Schmeikel had been staring at her husband with frightened eyes. Now she, too, sank on a chair, and nervously

80

drew her cardigan closer about her. Schmeikel grabbed at his corduroyed knees.

'So ask then. Ask! Ask away. We have our dinner at the hotel, yes? There is something criminal about that?'

Gently said: 'At the table next to you. Would you have noticed who was dining there?'

'At the table next? Oh yes, an old man! White hair and a field-coat, perhaps someone's old clerk. You are suspecting him?'

'He mentioned seeing you there.'

'So what is that? We are also seeing him.'

'He, of course, noticed that you spoke in German. That you were discussing some subject over your meal.'

Was there a quick intake of breath from Trudi Schmeikel? Her husband's eyes were riveted on Gently. He edged forward a little on the chair, his hands grabbing his knees a little tighter.

'He is overhearing us, then, this old man?'

'Merely that you appeared to be in earnest discussion.'

'He – speaks German?'

Gently paused long, then gave a single shake of his head. Schmeikel tossed his own.

'Then, no matter! It is affairs of business we speak.'

'Affairs of business?'

'Of no concern! But we would not wish them overheard.'

Gently paused again, and nodded. 'You took your coffee in the lounge, I believe,' he said.

'And it is this same old man who tells you? Every movement of ours he watches?'

'He remembers that.'

Schmeikel's eyes were locked to his. 'I do not like this,' he said. 'I do not like it. So yes, we go to the lounge, and this we do not mention in our statement. Is it then some very great matter that we drink coffee here, and not there?'

'A simple question of fact.'

'This man, he is spying on us? I do not recall seeing him in the lounge. I cannot think he is a reliable witness.'

'He heard you order your coffee to be served there.'

'And that is all?'

'That is all.'

Was there a flicker in the brown eyes? Trudi Schmeikel was gripping her hands tightly.

'So,' Schmeikel said. 'So. We are spending a quiet hour in the lounge. It is not yet time to meet Uncle Gunther and we do not wish to encounter the peasants. Is this then culpable?'

'Were other guests present?'

'Who, I will leave to your enquiry.'

'Yes, yes, there were other people there!' Trudi Schmeikel broke in. 'All the time. Until we left.'

'Until you left?'

'Yes!'

Schmeikel sent his wife a warning glare. She tugged nervously at her hands. 'Until – until we left,' she said.

'And that was – when?'

She looked at Schmeikel.

'You were told,' Schmeikel said. 'We left at ten. To meet Uncle Gunther at the quay at ten fifteen. This you will find in our statement.'

'Precisely at ten?'

'A minute more, a minute less! In the end, what does it matter? When we arrive it is too late, there is no Uncle Gunther on the quay.'

'When you arrived.'

'Yes, I am saying!'

'When you and your wife arrived at the quay.'

'Must I repeat this?'

'Both you. And your wife.'

Schmeikel stared and stared. And so did Trudi Schmeikel.

Gently said to Schmeikel: 'When we discussed this

earlier you remembered a car that passed you, but your wife was unable to remember it. We have since been successful in tracing that car.'

At last, a flicker in those eyes? Trudi Schmeikel was gazing at her lap. Schmeikel snapped:

'But there were many cars! What has this car to do with us?'

Gently said: 'We have spoken to the driver.'

'So?'

'He was the gentleman who sat next to you at dinner.'

'Him!'

Gently nodded.

'I am having enough of this!' Schmeikel rapped. 'He is spying here, he is spying there, and who shall believe a word he says? What new lies has he been telling?'

Gently said: 'He also remembers the encounter.'

'Of course! And then?'

'He saw you plainly in his headlights.'

'And. And?'

'He saw you alone. Alone and proceeding towards the quay.'

'*Ach*, the crazy old liar!' Schmeikel's fists pounded his knees. 'And you have paid him? You have paid him for this? He is perhaps one of your criminal informants?'

Slowly, Gently shook his head.

'Then, it is for kicks he tells you this! Oh yes, his type we have met. He is getting his thrill, and cares nothing for the consequences. But ha, ha, no. It will not do. You are not such a fool, Herr Superintendent.'

Gently said: 'Did you go there alone, Schmeikel?'

'Ask me – ask my wife!'

Gently looked across at Trudi Schmeikel, whose eyes remained fixed on her lap.

'Well?'

'We – we go there together!' Her hands twisted and twisted.

83

'Together you left the hotel?'

'Yes!'

'And together walked down to the quay?'

'Yes. Oh yes!'

Gently paused. 'You can be quite certain of that, Frau Schmeikel?'

'She has told you!' Schmeikel snarled. 'She tells you, I tell you, kindly you will leave my wife alone.'

Gently said: 'Frau Schmeikel?'

'Oh please, yes!' Trudi Schmeikel burst into tears. Schmeikel jumped to his feet.

'Enough!' he snarled. 'Enough. This shall go to the Embassy, Herr Gently. It is plain. You are trying to frame me. You will bring false witness. But no. But no.'

Gently stared at the flushed, twitching face. 'Please sit down, Herr Schmeikel,' he said.

'You are trying, but it shall not be!'

'Then, if you prefer, you may stand.'

Schmeikel glared and glared. 'I wish to speak to my Embassy,' he said. 'It is my right, you cannot deny me. I will speak to my Embassy. And it shall be now.'

'Oh, Willi, Willi!' Trudi Schmeikel sobbed.

'Kindly hand me that phone,' Schmeikel said.

'Willi, oh Willi!'

Gently reached for the phone and pushed it across the desk. Schmeikel grabbed it. He drew his chair up. He pulled a card from a fat wallet and keyed a number with a stabbing finger. Then he sat back complacently with the phone to his ear.

'*Die Gesandtschaft*? Herr Wilhelm Schmeikel . . .'

The rest of the conversation was in German. At first it was abrupt and impatient: he was probably being handed from one recipient to another; then it settled down to an indignant monologue in which the word *polizei* and Gently's name were freely interchanged. Meanwhile Trudi Schmeikel snivelled into a handkerchief and occasionally burst out into sobs again. Once or twice Schmeikel snarled some remark at her but the tears didn't cease to flow. Then the monologue began to be broken, and Schmeikel's indignation to grow. There were long silences, punctuated with snarls; and finally a subdued response spoken through clenched teeth. Then Schmeikel slammed the instrument down.

'*Gott im Himmel* – they are worse than you!' He stared ferociously at the phone. 'They do not care. They do not care!'

'Oh Willi!' Trudi Schmeikel wailed. 'We must do it. We must do what they say!'

'I will write to the Minister, yes. With this they shall not get away.'

'Willi, it is best!'

Schmeikel snarled in German and continued to disintegrate the phone with his eyes.

Gently said: 'You were offered advice?'

'Oh yes, advice!' Trudi Schmeikel wailed. 'We are to remain here in this place. We must give you all the assistance we can.'

'That would seem sensible.'

'Sensible, yes.' But Trudi Schmeikel threw a fearful look at her husband.

'And advice I trust you will follow.'

Still through his teeth, Schmeikel snarled: 'Do we have an option?'

Gently returned the phone to its place. He said: 'Am I to take it that the witness I spoke to was mistaken?'

'He is mistaken, he is blind, he is a liar. And he is all these things three times over.'

'Together, you left the hotel.'

'Once more!'

'And together arrived at the quay.'

'In a moment, I spit!'

'And that goes for both of you?'

85

Schmeikel's eyes blazed at Trudi. Trudi sank her head.

'In that case, I will detain you no longer.'

Schmeikel said: 'I do not want your car. We shall walk. And if I have influence yet with the Ministry, there are those here who will rue this moment.'

He got to his feet, and pulled his wife to hers. Slatter jumped up and saw them through the door. When they were gone, Aspall slid a look at Gently. He said:

'I don't know, sir. But I think we've had one liar in here tonight!'

After a pause Gently nodded.

'If we could get that missus of his on her own, sir. I was watching her. I'm sure she'd spill. She was only just keeping her end up back there.'

'She's standing by him.'

'You're right, sir. And I don't think it's going to last for ever.'

Gently said: 'We need a lead from the hotel. It's becoming clear that he left there without her. If the staff can't tell us anything we shall have to track down customers who were present last night.'

'I'll put men on it,' Aspall said. 'I want that Boche. It's getting kind of personal between him and us.'

Gently shrugged. 'It's beginning to build. But we mustn't let it run away with us quite yet.'

Aspall shook his head. 'He's kosher for me, sir.' Then his eyes were serious. He said: 'You don't think that Ministry of his can spring him – something political, like that?'

'I think it unlikely.'

Aspall looked at the phone. 'I would take that as personal,' he said. 'But the Embassy, they seem to be on our side. I don't think they like him any better than we do.'

Before leaving, Gently rang his housekeeper to tell her to expect him. The mist was thick when he took to the road. His route to Heatherings took him past Grange Farm, but no light was visible at the end of the lane. But then, there were pigs to be fed in the morning, and the hens whose eggs Bert Moulton had once purloined.

6

'That confounded Embassy has been on my neck again. How close are we to an arrest, Gently?'

Gently had been at the point of going to his car the next morning when the Assistant Commissioner rang.

Outside a ghostly sun was beginning to peer through the mist that clung to The Walks, and down the garden, the odd-job man was barrowing leaves to the compost heap. Gently had arrived back late the night before, but Mrs Jarvis had been waiting for him with a hot meal. Before sitting down to that, however, he had put a call through to Rouen.

'You are at Heatherings? You lucky man!'

In Rouen it had apparently rained all day. Gabrielle had been out to the china factory selecting stock for the Christmas trade, and had arrived back at the house at Mont St Aignan very damp, and feeling rather depressed. Then, she had rung an empty flat! Wasn't there some law that made it inevitable? And now she was learning that her man was at home, while she was stranded in streaming Rouen. It wasn't fair, *non*, *non*, and what did she care for these foolish yachtsmen?

Mrs Jarvis, who'd suffered raids in Finchley, took a keener interest in the affair. The local paper had made much of the victim's connection with the Luftwaffe and had even found up a photograph from somewhere. Over breakfast, Gently had studied it. Even in his seventies,

Gunther Herschfeldt was a handsome man, hawkish features, abundant grey hair, and an appealing twinkle in his bold eyes. And as a young man . . .? Gently remembered that bleak room with its rusting bedstead, the packing case beside it, the lamp still containing a cupful of paraffin. Fifty years since. One could begin to understand the tragic fate of poor Molly Hardyment.

'Listen, Gently. The nephew. I take it he's our man?'

'There just could be other factors . . .'

The AC made impatient noises. 'Forget the other factors, and listen to this one! The Embassy were reluctant to mention it, but there's an investigation going on in Germany. And the gist of it is that Schmeikel is a wrong'un. He's been authorising payments to mysterious accounts. So if we don't want him, they do. But it's plain why they felt obliged to draw it to our attention. Are you with me?'

Gently was with him.

'Then what's the score? How close are we?'

Gently said: 'We are near an arrest, but we still need the testimony of a critical witness.'

'How blasted critical?'

'It relates to Schmeikel's movements. Without it, the charge may not stick.'

'And are you likely to crack it?'

'I think it probable. The locals are pulling out the stops on it now.'

More impatient noises! 'Crack the whip, Gently. I want this little business cleared up promptly. And if it needs a word in the ear of the DPP, well, you only have to give me the wink.'

Gently hung up; then lifted the phone again and rang the Harford police station number. Aspall had arrived. Gently said:

'Anything in from the hotel?'

'We've found a couple of customers who were in the

lounge, sir, but the Schmeikels were still there when they left.'

Gently said: 'I'm just leaving, and I'd like a word with Schmeikel first thing. Will you fetch him in?'

'Right away, sir,' Aspall said. He paused. 'Has something turned up, then?'

'Something,' Gently said. 'It will keep.'

He collected his car and left. Significant it had to be, that information passed on from the Embassy. Trudi Schmeikel knew the score, he was certain: it was about this that Stratton had observed them arguing in the hotel, when Schmeikel had been trying to shut her up. There, and in the lounge later, had probably been the crisis point of the affair. What had he told her? That he was going to confess, to throw himself on his uncle's mercy? That for this he needed to see Herschfeldt alone, and that she must stay behind to give him the opportunity? Probably. And that interview on the quay . . . had Herschfeldt, fatally, decided that Schmeikel's offence was beyond forgiveness, that action must follow, Schmeikel be sacked, and the will, of course, revised? Gently gazed at the road ahead. And afterwards, what had Schmeikel told his wife? That he had arrived to find the quay deserted . . . no sign of Herschfeld, no sign of his assassin?

He passed the turn-off to Grange Farm, where the house showed whitely for a moment. Colour was returning as the mist dissolved, ahead the church tower and castle keep of Harford stood proud on the horizon.

Could she believe him, knowing what she knew? Clearly Trudi Schmeikel was a very disturbed woman. In the end, would the burden be too much, would her deadly testimony conclude the affair?

He drove into the village, into the square, and parked beside a couple of patrol cars. Through the window of the police station's office he could see Aspall gesticulating to

90

the phone. He went in. Bartram was at the desk. He rose to his feet anxiously as Gently entered. Gently said:

'Has Schmeikel been fetched?'

'We did go after him, sir!' Bartram said.

Gently stared at him. 'And?'

'The bugger's gone,' Bartram said. 'Yacht and all.'

'Did no one see the yacht leave?'

In the office, Aspall had hung up the phone with a slam. He sat for a moment staring, his hands working dementedly. Slatter stood by with a cautious expression. He said:

'It was me who went for him, sir. I did ask an old fellow who was hanging out nets, but the yacht had gone before he got there.'

'The bastard!' Aspall burst out. 'He probably took off straight away last night. We should have had him in a cell. He'll be half-way across to Holland by now.'

'Don't think it was last night, sir,' Slatter ventured. 'Not with all that fog about. He'd have run into those moored yachts, or maybe put himself aground.'

'I wouldn't put it past him!'

'More like first light, sir. Could be he's still working his way downriver. Then there's the tide. I asked the fisherman. He said it was slack water, would soon be flooding.'

'And what the devil does that mean?'

'Means he's heading into it, won't be making so much ground.'

Aspall swore. 'I've rung the coastguard,' he said. 'And they're getting on to Fishery Protection. They'll send a patrol boat up the coast, so there's a chance we'll get our hands on him yet.'

Gently said: 'Can we have a map?'

'Bartram!' Aspall shouted.

A map was fetched and spread out on the desk. It showed the Harford River winding its way to the sea. A narrow peninsula of sand dunes hemmed it from the sea and at one point it divided round a marshy island. Then there was a modest tributary wriggling inland to a small village. The country about was low marshes where roads were few, hair-like and uncoloured. Gently pointed to the village.

'Send a patrol there. Then get me the Mariners on the phone.'

Aspall hastened to obey. Moments later Gently was connected with Shavers.

'Chiefie, that bleeding Kraut has cleared off – !'

'Shut up, Shavers, and just listen. Is that inflatable of yours still in commission?'

'Well yes, Chiefie – '

'I shall need it. Get it tanked up and ready to go. We'll be down there in a few minutes.'

'But Chiefie, it costs a bit – !'

'Just do it. Money we can talk about later.'

He hung up. Aspall was staring. 'You – you're really going after him, sir?'

Gently nodded. 'Slatter is right. If Schmeikel ventured out last night, then he's probably aground. If he went this morning, then he's punching the flood, and Shavers' inflatable has a chance of catching him.'

'But . . . if he's got to the sea?'

'Then it's up to the Navy. But the odds are he's somewhere down the river. Is there anyone here who can handle a yacht?'

'I can, sir,' Slatter said. 'I've got my own boat round at Pin Mill.'

Together with a uniform man they drove down to the now-empty quay. There they found Shavers at the dinghy mooring, funnelling petrol into the outboard of his inflatable.

92

'Chiefie, there's my time too – '

'Later.'

'This bleeding juice doesn't come cheap!'

Gently brushed his protests aside and, along with the other two, climbed into the inflatable. Slatter cast off and shoved them clear, and Shavers got the engine running. The tide was now in full flood but the inflatable skipped over it at a useful clip. Buoys, yachts sped towards them, the quay and the village receded astern. Ahead the river split two ways, with a subsidiary channel to port.

'Which way round the island, Chiefie?'

'If you were a yacht, which way would you go?'

'Not through the sodding narrows I wouldn't!'

'So.'

Shavers headed for the starboard channel.

Yet, if what one had heard of Schmeikel's seamanship were true . . .? Gently stared long at the alternative route. But the die was cast, and the port channel quickly vanished as they bore away behind the island. Slatter said:

'It's almost a flat calm, sir. He won't get far if he's short of juice.'

But Herschfeldt had probably taken care of that: he had planned to sail the following day.

Reach followed reach. They met no other boats from whom to enquire of the fugitives. On either hand the horizon stopped at the level of reeds and dead rushes. Finally the tributary river arrived . . . could Schmeikel have taken refuge there? And then they were done with the island and pointing down the last long stretch to the sea.

'How much further?'

'There's two miles of this, Chiefie.'

But ahead, no sign of moving masts. And in a landscape so very flat, must they not be seeing them, if they were there? Then:

'Sir!'

Slatter was gazing behind them, where the alternative channel joined the main stream. At the point of the island grew a few scrub willows, and, somewhere behind them . . .

'Turn the boat!'

Shavers throttled down and swung the inflatable about. Now, with the flood under it, it seemed to be positively flying on its new course.

'It's got to be her, sir – the twin masts. And they're not moving – he's put her aground!'

'The silly bugger!' Shavers exclaimed. 'Taking her down that way on the ebb!'

He ported his helm, and they surged into the channel. Now the situation was becoming plain. Still distant, and near the centre of the channel, the *Electra* was stuck with her bows pushing high. On the cabin roof sat a disconsolate figure. It jumped to its feet as it spotted the inflatable. Then a tiny head poked up from the well, and moments later water surged from beneath the yacht's stern.

'The sod won't get her off like that! He's been and stuck her on the Hen and Chickens.'

'It'll need another hour of the flood,' Slatter said. 'Maybe longer, the way she's lying.'

The inflatable flew on. As they drew closer, the surge from the *Electra*'s stern ceased. One of the figures went below: Schmeikel alone stood watching them approach. His gaze was stony. Shavers cut his engine; the inflatable drifted in beside the yacht. Slatter took the painter and stepped aboard, followed by Gently and the uniform man. Schmeikel remained silent. Gently said:

'It is unfortunate that you have taken this action, Herr Schmeikel. You must regard yoursèlf as being under arrest. And that applies also to this vessel.'

'Under arrest!'

'As from this moment.'

'*Ach*, but my Embassy shall hear of this!'

'I believe they are eager to be informed,' Gently said.
Schmeikel stared hard. And from the cabin came a wail.

It took the full hour for the tide to rise high enough to
release the *Electra* from the Hen and Chickens' embrace,
and then, on Shavers' advice, they set a course downstream, rather than retrace the narrow channel. The
Schmeikels remained in the cabin, occasionally muttering
to each other in German. Slatter managed the helm, with
an occasional hint from a cock-a-hoop Shavers. Because
the Krauts were getting their deserts, weren't they? And
he, Shavers, had had a big hand in it! He spent the trip
sprawled on a bench in the well, a malicious smirk on his
face.

It was near noon when the yacht was returned to her
moorings and Shavers and his inflatable dismissed. Sul-
lenly, Schmeikel climbed up from the cabin to be escorted
to the car by Slatter and the uniform man. Then Trudi
Schmeikel emerged. She stood as though tongue-tied
before Gently. At last she faltered:

'And – also me? I, too, am being arrested?'

Gently stared long, then shook his head.

'But if he is guilty, shall not I be?'

'Your husband is guilty of disobeying police
instructions.'

'Of – disobeying?'

Gently nodded. Trudi Schmeikel's lips were quivering.
She said:

'But I do not understand! It is for this that you arrest
him?'

'He was required to remain in Harford.'

'It is – this?'

Gently said nothing. Trudy Schmeikel's blue eyes were
very large.

'And – for me?'

'The same instructions apply. Until the enquiry is complete you must remain in Harford. You may stay on the yacht if you wish, or, if you prefer it, transfer to the hotel.'

She shivered. 'No. I shall remain here.'

'At the hotel your expenses will be paid.'

She shook her head wildly. 'Here I shall be. Do not fear – I cannot manage this boat! But – I may see Willi?'

'That can be arranged.'

Tears were welling in the blue eyes. She said: 'It is not true, Willi did not do this terrible thing. Please, you must believe this! Of such things he cannot be capable.'

'Do you believe it, Frau Schmeikel?'

'Yes, I believe – I believe!'

'Yet . . .?'

'It is true – true!'

Now the tears had become sobs. Suddenly, Trudi Schmeikel broke away from him. She tumbled down the stairs into the cabin and threw herself on a bunk. There she remained, face down, sobbing, her blonde hair tangled about her. Gently went. Slatter had come back.

'So what was that all about, sir?' he said, as they walked over the quay.

But Gently merely shook his head.

In the car, Schmeikel sat with his grim face averted.

In the office they gave him a mug of coffee, which he drank with an expression of distaste. Aspall, forewarned on the car's radio, had already called off the hunt for the yacht. Taking him aside, Gently briefed him on the information that had come from town, and the gleeful Aspall rubbed his hands and darted eager little looks at the man sitting in the office.

'Do you think he'll cough, sir?'

'I very much doubt it.'

'But when he hears we know what you've just told me?'

'I think it more likely he'll keep his mouth tight shut.'

'But after a sweat in the cell, sir?'

Gently shrugged.

Surprisingly, however, after his spell with the coffee, Schmeikel had begun to look a good deal less dour. He rose to his feet when they re-entered the office, and even managed the ghost of an ingratiating smile. His hand waved in an expansive gesture.

'Herr Gently, is it not time we were talking?'

'Please do be seated, Herr Schmeikel.'

'Of course, of course! But should we not confer together on this sad affair?'

'You wish to make a statement?'

'*Ach*, not like that! It is together, you and I, who should be speaking – you, the Herr Superintendent who was sent to take charge, and myself, the most closely interested. Is it not so?'

Gently stared at him. 'You are suggesting I give you a private interview?'

'But yes. We do not need these under-strappers. It is best that we approach this man to man.'

'You mean – without witnesses?'

'Between ourselves, all. Afterwards you may make of it what you will.' His eyes fixed on Gently's. 'There are, perhaps, matters confidential, which, to the underlings, I shall not speak.'

Gently stared at him for a very long time. He said: 'I don't think you quite understand your position, Herr Schmeikel. You are under arrest for disobeying a police injunction, issued in connection of yourself with a serious crime.'

He threw out his hand. 'Understood, understood! Such a man as yourself must go by the book. But to clear this matter up briefly, yes? To waste no more time? I think it is best.'

Gently said: 'Does this involve a confession?'

'*Nein*! No confession. I have none to make.'

'No confession.'

Schmeikel shook his head. 'Between you and me. A confidential exchange.'

'A bit irregular, sir,' Aspall said stoutly. 'Should have one of us in on it at least.'

'Then,' Schmeikel said, 'my lips are sealed. I have no more to say to you at all.'

'All the same, sir,' Aspall said.

Gently sighed. He looked at Aspall. 'Perhaps if you and the constable will step outside?'

'Well . . . I don't know, sir!'

'If you would.'

After a pause, Aspall jerked himself to his feet and signalled to the uniform man who'd been attending Schmeikel. The door closed.

'Is better,' Schmeikel said. 'Now we can talk man to man.' He drew his chair closer to the desk. 'You have heard, then? The Embassy informs you?'

Slowly, Gently lit his pipe. Schmeikel watched for a moment, then felt in his pocket. He drew out a cigar. He looked at Gently.

'It is all right, yes?'

'You may smoke.'

Schmeikel lit his cigar and blew a cloud over Gently. 'So,' he said. 'This I am expecting. The rabbit is out. And alone I must face it.'

'Alone . . .?'

'But of course. Uncle Gunther is no longer with us. So all we are doing – and it is quite legal – must be placed to the account of wicked Willi.'

Gently said: 'I understand money has been illegally transferred.'

'*Ach*, they will say that!' Schmeikel blew smoke. 'But not so. It is as you say, above the board. These things I am doing with Uncle Gunther's full knowledge.'

'You are blaming your uncle?'

'There is no blame!' Schmeikel drew furiously on the cigar. 'You do not understand, it is not your *métier*, but things are not well with our famous industry. The market is flooded, production is down, in other directions we have been looking. For this, we set capital aside, we build a reserve to fund other ventures. It is confidential, oh yes, we cannot be telling all the world.'

'And these transfers were known by only two people?'

Schmeikel nodded. 'And now, alas, by only one.'

'Who may have difficulty in proving their legality.'

'No, no!' He slammed his cigar on the ashtray. 'It is my absence that matters, can you not see? Over there are people who wish me ill. I must be in Lübeck, I must be at the helm, for this only I am seeking to set sail. Can you not sympathise?'

Gently blew smoke.

'It is essential in every way,' Schmeikel said. 'My honour is in question, and a major firm, and many . . .' He paused. '. . . very many marks.' He paused again. 'We deal in millions,' he said. 'A million of marks is good money.'

Gently blew smoke. Schmeikel also.

'Now you are understanding,' he said. 'And why are we kept here? No reason! All we can tell you has been told. For me, it is twice a tragedy that Uncle Gunther is no more, but if he dies as you say, then there are suspects to hand in plenty. The peasants, yes? Perhaps no proof, but suspicion very strong. And others.' Schmeikel shrugged. 'It does not matter who they are.'

Gently said: 'I should choose a scapegoat?'

'*Ach*, no! I am just saying. It may be no culprit will come to hand, so what then? The case is closed.'

Gently blew smoke.

'Is understood?' Schmeikel said.

Gently said: 'There may be a problem.'

Schmeikel waved his cigar. 'A problem! For such a man as yourself, what is that?'

Gently blew smoke. Schmeikel lowered his voice. 'Listen,' he said, leaning closer. 'In *Die Schweiz* a bank, yes? I lift that phone, ring a certain number, give instructions which you shall hear. Then to you I hand the phone, and certain details you will write down. And you give instructions. And wait. And next your own bank you will ring. And it is good, it is above the board, already your instructions have been obeyed.'

Gently blew smoke.

'Is simple, yes?'

'Very simple.'

Schmeikel drew even closer. 'And we do not talk peanuts, Herr Gently, I am thinking those marks should be pounds sterling. A good round figure, yes? One million of pounds sterling. You tell me, I pick up the phone, and minutes later such a sum is your own.'

Gently said: 'Yet there is this problem.'

Schmeikel waved his cigar. 'This is for you!'

Gently shook his head. 'The problem is yourself. And how you can be presented as an innocent party.'

'How . . .?'

Gently nodded. He leaned back in his chair and regarded Schmeikel. He said: 'The culprit in this case required a motive. And plainly the strongest possible motive pertains to you.'

'To me? But I am telling you – !'

Gently bowed. 'And I note your assertions. But to others it may appear a powerful objection to considering you as an innocent man. In addition you had opportunity. And today, apparently, you sought to escape the process of justice. Altogether, it creates an appearance which I would find it difficult to ignore.'

Schmeikel stared with arrested cigar. 'But – a man like yourself?'

Gently shrugged. 'I cannot change facts.'

'But . . . facts can be presented, yes?'

'Unfortunately these facts are too well established.'

Schmeikel stared some more. 'Listen, Englishman!' He violently stubbed out the cigar. 'So, one million is not enough, ha? The bargain is not yet to your satisfaction! Shall it be two? Perhaps more? Is that why the difficulties you make?'

Gently said: 'In hot money?'

'In hot, in cold, what is that to you?'

'It perhaps adds another fact.'

Schmeikel's eyes were blazing. He snarled: 'Then, no deal?'

Gently merely stared back.

'*Gott im Himmel*! Give me that phone!'

Gently pushed the phone across to him. Schmeikel seized it and began to dial, then as violently slammed it down again.

'Englishman, one last time . . .!'

'Make your phone call, Herr Schmeikel.'

'You cannot be so stupid!'

'A man under arrest is allowed to make one.'

Schmeikel's thick lips were working. He stared at the phone as though it might bite him. He didn't make the call. Eventually, Gently pressed the bell on the desk.

'That slimy so-and-so, sir! Trying to buy you off with nicked money!'

Schmeikel had been escorted to the station's single cell, leaving the smell of his cigar to linger in the office. He had gone reluctantly, requiring assistance, and snarling threats at his escort in German. Aspall had returned dusting his hands and sniffing disgustedly at the unwonted odour.

'You listened, of course.'

'You bet, sir! Slatter and me had our ears to the door. So we can do him for that too if nothing else sticks. But he's got it coming, that Kraut. Him going on a flyer about ties it up. And it's going to be a real pleasure to put him on the hooks.'

Gently said: 'We still haven't nailed him.'

Aspall jiggled his shoulders. 'It can't take much more, sir! Not with a motive like he's got. That funny business back home is going to do for him!'

'He claims it is legal. And that his uncle was privy to it.'

'Well, he would say that, sir, wouldn't he?'

'Until we know for certain, we can't depend on it.'

Aspall grimaced. 'I can't see a jury giving him the benefit of the doubt!'

'We could still use that extra witness.'

'Well, I don't know,' Aspall said. 'We've got him going towards the quay, with his uncle waiting for him, and him with everything to play for. Everyone else has gone home and Shavers is safe back in his kitchen. If it wasn't the Kraut, then who was it? I can't see any room for a mystery man.'

Gently drew on a dead pipe. Was he, perhaps, being too cautious? In his mind he was seeing that picture of Frau Schmeikel sobbing prostrate on the berth. Did she know, or merely suspect? Of her husband's financial entanglements she must have an idea. And apparently she had been a willing assistant in his recent attempt to get away. And yet . . .? Was there still some loophole, however small, in the case against Schmeikel?

'We must be able to show he left the hotel alone.'

'We're doing our best, sir. But it isn't easy. The staff can't help us, and so far we've only traced those two regulars.'

'But between the hotel and where Stratton saw him?'

102

'The men have been pretty thorough. Only after ten on a foggy old night there weren't many people about.'

Gently sighed. 'And nothing fresh has come in?'

About to shake his head, Aspall hesitated. 'While you were down the river we got a call from Wolmering, but it was about Sunday, just filling in.'

'About the Schmeikels?'

'Herschfeldt, sir. One of our lot from Wolmering saw the picture in the paper. Remembered he'd seen him at the bird reserve on Sunday. He thought he saw him talking to Mr Stratton.'

'To Stratton?'

'That's what he says, though he could have been mistaken. Anyway, he decided to give us a ring, just in case it was any use to us.'

'Stratton . . .' Gently said.

'Probably got it wrong, sir. Or Mr Stratton would have mentioned it.'

Gently thought about it then shrugged. The clock on the wall said it was lunchtime. He knocked out his pipe, and rose.

'If anything comes up, I'm in the Castle Arms,' he said.

The hotel occupied a corner site at the far angle of the square, where it neighboured closely the tall tower and sloping mead of the castle keep. It was fronted by the trees and shrubbery of a house at the end of the square, and the road extended to bear left around the hotel's walled grounds. On the other side an alley separated it from buildings lining the square, which included a couple of small shops and a modest restaurant advertising sea-food. On the steps Gently paused to take in the scene, but even at that hour the neighbourhood was almost deserted. While, after ten, on a foggy old night . . .? After a moment he shrugged, and went on into the hotel.

'You're here for lunch, sir?'

The bar was to the right, with ornate sash windows facing the trees. Adjacent was the dining-room, with a similar outlook, and there the windows were hung with looped-back velvet curtains.

'Which is the lounge?'

'I'm afraid you're too late for morning coffee, sir.'

'Still . . .?'

'Straight through, sir.' The waitress pointed down the hall.

Gently went through, passing an ornate staircase below which a door led to toilets. The lounge was a pleasant, panelled room with french doors that opened on to a lawn. Beyond that again was the hotel car-park, sur-rounded by a brick wall. Gently tried the french doors. They were unlocked. He took a few steps out on the lawn. A gravel path led to the car-park and passed a door let into the outer wall. The door was bolted: Gently unbolted it. It gave on the alley that ran beside the hotel. He rebolted the door and returned to the hotel.

'Is it lunch, sir?'

'First, I'll have a drink.'

In the bar there were only a handful of customers. A tall, blonde barmaid drew him a pint of Adnams and smilingly set it before him.

'You're the man down from London, sir?'

Gently nodded. He said: 'Who is in charge of the garden and car-park?'

'That's Les, sir. Did you want to talk to him?'

Gently sipped. 'If he isn't too busy.'

Les was called. He was a smallish, bright-eyed man wearing a cap and dungarees. He came in rubbing a pair of grubby hands, and gave Gently's glass a meaningful look. Gently said:

'Yesterday morning. Would you have checked that door into the alley?'

'Oh, ah!' Les ducked his head guiltily. 'I thought someone would be on to me about that.'

'You found it unbolted?'

'You seem to know. But I can't think how it happened. The governor is hot about security, and I'll swear I checked that bugger last thing.'

'But you found it unbolted.'

'Some sod must have done it.'

'At what time would you have made your check?'

'W'like I told you, last thing. I get away from here about six most nights.' He sent the barmaid a quick look. 'Do Harry know?'

'Hasn't said anything,' the barmaid said.

'He'll give me a rollicking,' Les said. 'And it wasn't my fault, that I'll swear. Do you have to tell him, guv?'

Gently shook his head. 'But I may need a statement from you,' he said.

'Oh ah, you'll be one of them there,' Les said ruefully. 'It'll get around.'

'What will it be?' Gently said.

Les accepted a pint, and the barmaid a gin. She sipped. 'I suppose we mustn't ask you,' she said. 'But they do say you've pinched that bloke off the yacht. Him who was here with his wife on Tuesday.'

'You remember them?' Gently said.

The barmaid sipped. 'Didn't like him,' she said. 'The way he treated her. Think I'd have slung my drink in his face.'

'You didn't see them leave?'

She shook her head. 'I took them their coffee in the lounge. They were sitting by the window. He was going on at her. She was almost in tears, the poor woman.'

'Who else was in the lounge?'

'This couple from Thwaite. I told your blokes about them. Then there was a party of three, and a woman on her own. But no one I knew.'

'And you saw no more of them.'

'Didn't want to. After that I was giving a hand in here. Last thing I went in there to collect the cups and lock up, but they were gone by then.'

Gently drank. Les said:

'Is it right, then? Are you doing that bugger for the job?'

Gently drank. He said: 'What's on the menu?'

'Me, I'd try the pheasant,' the barmaid said.

Only a few tables were taken in the dining-room and Gently chose one with a view into the square. Across at the police station a patrol car was leaving, but that, for

the moment, was the only activity. He ordered the vegetable soup. It came with a crisp stick of French bread. He
was almost through it when a fresh movement in the
square caught his eye. A blue car – was it a Corsa? – was
manoeuvring into the parking, and a few moments later
there was no doubt: he saw the lean form of Stratton
climb out. The retired bank man locked his car, turned
and headed for the hotel. Gently heard the swing-doors
thud, and shortly after Stratton appeared in the dining-
room entry. His eye fell on Gently. He hesitated, then
advanced apologetically to Gently's table.

'Is it all right . . . may I?'

'Please do,' Gently said.

'I know I'm imposing, but – well! I've just come from
having a pint at the Mariners.'

'From the Mariners . . . ?'

'Yes. And you can guess what I've been hearing! And
there's something else I can tell you – about the man
there. Isn't his name Shavers?'

'Do sit down,' Gently said. 'And I can recommend the
vegetable soup.'

'It's so disturbing, all this,' Stratton said. 'I don't know.
I just couldn't keep away.'

He accepted Gently's recommendation and was served
with his bowl and French bread. He ate daintily but
nervously, his grey eyes occasionally flickering to
Gently's. Gently let him get on with it. After his soup, he
ordered the pheasant. It came with a pungent thick sauce
and a variety of choicely prepared vegetables. Stratton
followed suit, and willingly shared Gently's choice of
burgundy. As he ate, colour was mounting in his drawn,
sensitive face and his manner was becoming more relaxed.
At last he grounded his knife and fork tidily and took a
relishing mouthful from his glass.

'That was good! They have a knack with pheasant. I believe the secret is a dash of wine.'

Gently also drank, but made no comment. Stratton toyed with his glass, his eyes fixed on it. He said, lowering his voice:

'It's all over, then? You have charged the nephew?'

'We have made some progress.'

'But – after what happened? As you can imagine, I heard all about it down in the Mariners! That fellow Shavers was boasting unmercifully. You would have supposed he had captured the yacht on his own. By his account it's all sewn up, and the nephew is sitting in a cell awaiting his trial. Is there any truth in that?'

'The nephew is helping us.'

'In other words . . .?'

Gently said nothing.

'I'm only asking,' Stratton said, 'because I found myself wondering why Shavers was making such a song about it. One could almost sense a trace of relief in it, as though the way things had turned out was to his personal advantage.' He paused. 'Would that be possible?'

Gently said: 'You had something to tell me?'

'Yes.' Stratton studied his glass. 'Though it may be you already know it. So perhaps it doesn't matter anyway, if you are convinced that the nephew is the man.' He drank quickly. 'Shavers,' he said. 'The moment I saw him I knew. He was the man I saw at the quay, who was hanging about there as though waiting for someone. He disappeared, but heaven knows where, and there are plenty of places where he might have hidden. And then, this morning – well, I told you! I simply couldn't help wondering about the man.'

Gently said: 'We've talked to Shavers.'

Stratton paused. 'Was it him who told you about me?'

Gently nodded.

'So that's it,' Stratton said. 'No question that he was

down there. And whatever he says, he was acting suspiciously, as though he had something shady in mind. Has he given an explanation?'

Gently poured more wine.

'I know you can't tell me,' Stratton said. 'But listening to him down there I couldn't help feeling some doubts about him. And since it was I who put you on to the nephew, I felt it my duty to be frank about Shavers. He was there too, had equal opportunity.'

'Drink up,' Gently said. 'We'd better choose our sweet.'

'But mustn't it raise doubts about the guilt of the nephew?'

'I think the apple charlotte. Unless one prefers cheesecake.'

Stratton sighed softly, and desisted. Gently chose the apple charlotte, and Stratton some gâteau. Then came an admirable cheeseboard, and finally coffee and a bowl of mints. Stratton wiped his fingers on a serviette. He said:

'I still find it hard to believe the nephew guilty. I didn't like him. I thought him a boor. But that's a long way from being capable of such a deed as this. Can you be so certain?'

Gently took out his pipe. He said: 'Are you busy for the next hour?'

'Busy, no . . . and if you think I can help!'

'I would like you to drive me down to the quay.'

'To the quay – you mean, a reconstruction?'

'Something like that,' Gently said.

'Well, of course – I'd be only too pleased!'

But Stratton didn't look very greatly enthralled. He paid his bill, Gently noticed, from a well-filled wallet; but picked up his change and left no tip.

'There was a moon, you say.'

'Yes. Though the mist was getting thick down here.'

109

'No chance of seeing birds, then.'

'No, but you can hear them! I thought I explained that to you before.'

'Was it really worth it?'

'Yes. To one of us. But you'd need to be an enthusiast to understand.'

'To sit in your car on a cold night, for over an hour?'

'That's part of the game.'

They had fetched the Corsa, a current year model, and driven slowly down from the square. Then, at the quay, after careful thought, Stratton had parked on the upstream side, a couple of yards from the slipway. He'd placed the car on the slant; without turning one's head, one could glance towards the flood-ramp and the street. Ahead, one looked over the moorings. To the left, across the river to the marshy rond. A more deliberate twist of the head was needed to take in the fishermen's huts and the drawn-up boats.

Close by, the moored *Electra* looked very shut up indeed, with curtains drawn at the cabin windows and hatch and cabin doors firmly closed.

'You arrived here at nine.'

'Yes, I told you. There was nothing moving here then. And I opened my window just a fraction, so that I could hear if there was anything going on.'

'Could you hear the music from the Mariners?'

'No, thank heaven. It was just too far away. But I heard the birds I was telling you about.' He fumbled in the glove compartment. 'If my notebook was here, I could show you!'

'How long before Shavers turned up?'

'I didn't know who it was, then. I didn't hear him arrive, either, so he must have been very stealthy about it.'

'So when did you first see him?'

110

'At the most, ten minutes after I got here.'

'Show me where.'

Stratton pointed to the furthest corner of the quay. 'He suddenly appeared there, I don't know from where. I must have been looking across the river. I must admit his appearance startled me, because I hadn't heard a sound.'

'What was he doing?'

'Just standing there, looking at me as I thought. Then he turned himself about and seemed to be staring up the road. After that he began walking up and down, still giving looks in my direction. I think he was hoping I would clear off, and I very nearly did.'

'He gave you the impression of waiting for someone.'

'Yes, exactly that.'

'How long did he stay here?'

'Perhaps twenty minutes. But I can't say exactly when he left.'

'Another stealthy move?'

Stratton looked pained. 'This is the truth I'm trying to tell you! But yes, he must have picked the moment when I was straining to see those Brents come in. After that, there was no sign of him, it was literally as though he'd vanished.' Stratton paused. 'I suppose – it's just possible – that he could have dropped down into one of the dinghies?'

Gently looked at him and shrugged.

'Anyway, he couldn't have gone very far! There wasn't time. And my feeling was that he had gone into cover somewhere.'

'You saw no more of him.'

'No.' But Stratton seemed reluctant to dismiss Shavers. He stared hard at the shelter across from the quay, then over his shoulder at the fishermen's huts.

'So . . . then you had the quay to yourself for a while.'

'Yes. I suppose so.' Stratton frowned.

111

'Just you and the birds.'

'If you wish to put it like that. I wasn't aware of any other presence.'

'For the next half-hour.'

He nodded. 'But all the time the mist was thickening. In the end I could barely see the buildings over there. Some other person might well have been around.'

'But you saw no one. Until Herschfeldt came.'

Stratton's mouth was tight. 'No.'

'And his approach was far from stealthy.'

'Please, don't make fun of me!' Stratton begged. 'I told you, he was humming this tune, and strolling along, hands in pockets. He looked and acted like he was, a man who'd just come from a binge in a pub. I don't think he noticed me. He ambled across there and sat himself down on the bollard.'

Gently said: 'You didn't speak to him?'

'Speak to him – why would I?'

Gently shrugged. 'A fellow bird man?'

'A fellow . . . how was I to know that?'

Gently said: 'Didn't you have a word with him on Sunday, when he was visiting Grimchurch reserve?'

'I!'

'According to a witness, you were seen talking to him there.'

Stratton sat very still, staring straight ahead. At last he faltered: 'He . . . was that man?'

'You mean you didn't recognise him?'

'But no! It was misty, dark, he was just a figure.'

'Yet you tell me you could see the way he looked, and acted.'

'That was just an impression. I couldn't see who he was.'

'A man you'd spoken to two days before?'

'I can't help it! I didn't recognise him.'

Gently stared long, then shook his head. He said: 'Tell me about that encounter on Sunday.'

Stratton looked shaken. His mouth was twisting. He kept staring ahead at the yachts on the moorings. He said:

'It was crowded there, did they tell you? We had a rare bird drop in, and birders came from all over. I met one from Penzance, who'd driven all night, and another who'd flown down from Inverness. It was a lifer, a once in a lifetime bird, and the place was stiff with twitchers lugging cameras. And of course, I'm an officer in the local society, so a lot of them wanted a word with me.'

'Including Herschfeldt?'

'He – I don't know! I'd seen him talking to the Hardyments, earlier.'

Gently paused. 'You know the Hardyments?'

'Yes, of course. They used to be customers at the bank. Well, when they'd gone he – he approached me, asked me where he should go to see this bird. It was a type of heron, you know? And it had taken up quarters in what we call The Pulk. So I took him down to the stream and pointed out the way there. And then I went back to visit the hides, and that was really all I saw of him.'

'Yet, he was rather an unusual man.'

'Well – yes. I knew he wasn't English.'

'A striking appearance?'

Stratton hesitated. 'I – just saw him as another man of about my age.'

'In his early seventies.'

Stratton nodded.

'Another veteran of the war.'

'We didn't talk of that. We talked about birds.'

Stratton's hands were on the steering-wheel. He was holding it tightly.

Gently said: 'Where did you do your service?'

'Do we have to talk about that?' Stratton said. 'I was in

113

3 Group, and moved around a lot. In the end I was stationed in France.'

'3 Group?'

'Bomber Command.'

'Did that include Buxhall?'

'And if it did?'

Gently said: 'You will have read the local paper. Herschfeldt was shot down in a raid on Buxhall. Were you there at that time?'

Stratton bore down hard on the wheel. 'I was there and I wasn't there. At the time of the raids I was on leave in Eastwich, but I heard all about them when I got back. It wasn't any big thing. One fighter-bomber. Anti-personnel bombs and a couple of HEs. What was strange was he raided us three nights running. The rumour was that our boys had killed a relative of his.'

'So they were revenge raids.'

Stratton nodded.

'Was there much damage?'

'I didn't see much. The HEs blew a hole in a runway, but the butterfly bombs were soon tidied up.'

'Butterfly . . .?'

'Anti-personnel bombs. The casings flew open like wings. Then the lightest touch would set them off. But our bomb disposal squads knew how to handle them.'

'So . . . no casualties?'

'No casualties.' Stratton was still bearing down on the wheel.

Gently said: 'And the pilot of that plane. Was his identity known to you?'

Stratton shook his head. 'That was Army business. Ours stopped when we'd shot him down. The Army would have collected him and conducted the interrogation, and then passed on information to Command.'

'Nobody knew.'

'No.'

'And nobody met him. Then . . . or later.'

'Later?' The grey eyes turned to his with what seemed genuine incomprehension.

Gently said: 'In the latter part of the war POWs were lent out to farms. This was the case with Gunther Herschfeldt, and the occasion of his acquaintance with the Hardyments. He was on their farm in 1945, a farm within a stone's throw of RAF Buxhall. The Hardyments remember visits to the farm of RAF personnel. They appear to have been friends of a daughter. Named Molly.'

Still Stratton stared. The name seemed to mean nothing to him. He said: 'And this was in '45?'

Gently nodded.

'Then I'm afraid I can't help you. I was posted to Feltwell at the end of '44, and from there to a transit camp and France.'

'But you would have known the Hardyments?'

'I don't think so. Not until I met them as customers.'

'Perhaps the daughter? A dark girl? Said to have resembled Jessie Matthews?'

In the grey eyes, a sudden stillness. But immediately, Stratton shook his head. 'No. I don't remember her. I wasn't running around with girls much just then.'

'Molly,' Gently said. 'Molly Hardyment.'

'Oh, for heaven's sake!' Stratton exclaimed.

'She had a kiss-curl on her forehead.'

Stratton struck the wheel with both hands. 'Must we go on about this?' he said. 'I didn't know her, and that's all. And I didn't meet Herschfeldt when he was at the Hardyments'. Until Sunday I never knew of his existence.'

'Until Sunday.'

'Yes. And I didn't pay him much attention then. Or I would have known him again when I saw him, even on a dark and misty night.'

Gently shrugged. 'So let's get back to that, this unknown man sitting on the bollard.'

115

'I'm sorry,' Stratton said. 'But you upset me. You were touching a raw spot which you couldn't know about.' He ran a hand over his thinning white hair. 'I could see he was expecting someone,' he said. 'And I was about to give up, anyway. So a couple of minutes later I set off for home.'

'You started your motor,' Gently said. 'Then switched on your lights.'

'Yes, of course. Isn't that usual?'

'With the car positioned as it is now.'

'Yes.' Stratton stared hard ahead.

Gently said: 'You'd be looking straight at Herschfeldt. And Herschfeldt would be looking straight at you. The sound of the motor starting would have attracted his attention, and the lights have revealed him in full face. Surely you must have recognised him then?'

'No!'

'It seems impossible that you shouldn't. He was still sitting on the bollard?'

'Yes, yes!'

'While you were getting into gear, and releasing your brake?'

Stratton wrestled with the wheel. 'You don't under-stand! I'd only met him for five minutes. And no one was further from my thoughts. He was just one of the people I met on Sunday.'

'But . . . one who'd made an impression?'

'I can't think why!'

'A man of striking appearance. A foreigner. One you'd seen talking with your acquaintances, the Hardyments.'

'Oh, please!'

'Wasn't he someone rather special?'

Stratton hugged the wheel. 'Please – no! You can't understand. It's easy to talk like this now, but at the time . . . with the fog and everything . . .'

'Yet . . . you were looking straight at him.'

'No – I don't know! I was probably looking to see where I would make my turn. He was just a figure there, I had no reason to look at him. And if I'd seen who it was I wouldn't have wanted to stop.'

Gently shook his head.

'You believe me, don't you?'

Gently said: 'I'm trying to.'

'Then – you'll just have to think what you like!' And Stratton jerked his head round to stare at the flood-ramp.

Gently sighed. He'd neglected his pipe. Now he struck it a fresh light. Several times while they had been parked there, he'd seen a curtain twitch aboard the *Electra*. Other than that, and a distant figure by the huts, they had had the quay to themselves. He nostrilled smoke. He said:

'Now the lights are switched on, and you're making your turn. The man on the quay you're ignoring. Did your lights pick up anything else?'

'If you're not going to believe me – '

'Did they?'

Stratton twisted his mouth. 'No. And if you don't mind – '

'No sign of Shavers?'

'I'd like to say yes, but I didn't!'

'Perhaps further up? Towards the Mariners?'

'I've told you all about that before. I saw the nephew, proceeding alone, and nobody else. No one at all. And now – '

Exactly where was that?'

'It – perhaps fifty yards short of the Mariners!'

'As we drive back, perhaps you'll point it out.'

Irritably, Stratton turned the key in the ignition.

He pointed out the spot, but remained silent until they were parked again in the square. Then he turned quickly to Gently, an appealing look in his tired grey eyes. 'Look,' he said. 'I'm sorry. I know there's nothing personal in all this. You have a job to do, and you're doing it, and people

simply have to accept it. Only sometimes – you understand? There are sensitive areas in people's lives. Things
you may seem to deal with unfeelingly, though I'm sure
you have no such intention.'

Gently held the grey eyes. He said: 'Is there something
else you wish to tell me?'

Just for an instant, Stratton hesitated. Then he slowly
shook his head. He said: 'But the nephew . . . can you be
certain?'

'The enquiry is proceeding,' Gently said.

'Yes. I suppose so.'

Gently slipped his belt and climbed out of the car.

'So . . . that's one more nail in his coffin, sir!'

Gently found Aspall alone in the office. He had a plate
of sandwiches before him, along with the inevitable mug
of coffee.

'Has Schmeikel been fed?'

'We took him some food, sir, but somehow he doesn't
seem to have much appetite. He swore when Bartram
took it in, and said we'd all be sorry for this one day.'

Gently said: 'We can't be certain he made use of that
door.'

'But that'll be why no one saw him leaving the hotel,
sir. And that way he could say it was any old time, and
we could find no one to give him the lie.'

Gently said: 'And the lady?'

'Probably left the same way. After she'd given him time
to do the job.'

'In fact, she was his accomplice.'

'Must have been, sir. No other way.'

After a pause, Gently said: 'I've been talking to Stratton.' He gave Aspall a résumé of the conversation. The
local man listened with impatience and a growing
expression of incredulity. He swigged some coffee.

'I can't see much in that, sir. Not with an old buffer like Stratton.'

'He was there. He was alone with Herschfeldt. It is on his evidence that Schmeikel went to the quay on his own.'

'But this business with the girl, sir. It's a bit far-fetched.'

'He was stationed at Buxhall. He could have known her.'

'But fifty years ago, sir!'

Gently shrugged: perhaps fifty years did sound a little too long . . .

'I know we have to look at everything, sir,' Aspall said apologetically. 'But this one must be an outsider. We've got Schmeikel with everything going for him. Any minute now we could turn up the clincher.'

As though it had heard him, the phone rang, and Aspall swept it up. He listened with intent eyes, in which a gleam slowly began to form. 'Yes, ma'am . . . Right you are, ma'am . . . If you'll be good enough to do that.' He hung up the phone with a flourish and remained for a moment wth his hand resting on it.

'That was something?'

'A bit more than that, sir!' Aspall's hand caressed the phone. 'It was a call from a lady called Cartwright, who had coffee in the lounge at the Arms on Tuesday.'

'And she remembers the Schmeikels?'

Aspall nodded. 'She'll be over here in twenty minutes. Says she saw the Krauts go into the garden, and then the lady returning. The lady alone.'

8

'My name is Jessica Cartwright, Superintendent. In fact, we've met each other before. I was a form mistress at Huntingfield when you came there to interview Sweffy – Miss Swefling, I should have said! – who was our Head at that time. Since then she has moved to Scarborough, while I, of course, am retired.'

She thrust out her hand, a bold-faced lady dressed in a colourful costume with a low, sweeping skirt. Her bushy hair had been tinted auburn and she wore a treble rope of chunky amber. She smiled at Gently with determined eyes, and hoisted a chair closer to the desk.

'You still reside at Wolmering, Mrs Cartwright?'

'No, at Thwaite – and it's Miss, not Mrs! I felt I'd had enough of God's waiting-room, and I wanted to play my part in the Festival. I taught music, you understand, and now I'm on the Festival committee, so I found myself a cottage in Thwaite. Just across from the concert hall is where you'll find me.' She smiled brightly at Gently, at Aspall.

'So, on Tuesday night . . .?'

'Yes.' She nodded. 'I had Babs Makepeace staying with me.'

'Babs . . .?'

'A former colleague. These days she's living in Cambridge.'

'And you and she . . .?'

'Just a minute! I'm trying to explain why I only just got here. Yesterday I drove Babs home, and of course she would have me spend the night. I got back for a late lunch and it was then I saw the local paper – how the police would like to talk to anyone who dined at the Castle Arms on Tuesday.' She smoothed her skirt. 'So here I am. I took Babs there on her last evening. And having read the account of what happened, I can guess pretty well why you need my testimony. May I smoke?'

Gently nodded. Miss Cartwright fished a cigarette from her handbag. Gently struck her a light. 'Thanks.' She drew composedly on the cigarette. 'And it was him – that fellow – who you're after?'

Gently said: 'Just tell me what occurred.'

'Yes. Of course.' She frowned for a moment. 'I suppose we arrived there around six thirty, and went into the bar for a sherry. While we were there this fellow came in, trailing his poor little mouse of a wife. He ordered a pint, and she had a gin-sling, and they sat down at a table in the alcove. Babs thought they were Dutch, but I know a bit of German. Not that we tried to overhear their conversation.'

'But . . . a few words?'

'A few. The name "Gunther" cropped up all the time. Also – ' she shrugged – 'it was only an impression. But I got the idea that they were talking about money.'

'About money.'

'Yes. Finance. Banks, trusts – that sort of thing. Only please remember that my German is limited. I may have got hold of the wrong end of the stick.'

Gently said: 'Did they appear apprehensive?'

She exhaled smoke. 'The blonde mouse did. Not him. He did most of the talking. She was there mostly to provide him with an audience.' She paused. 'Come to

121

think of it, she didn't look particularly well. I noticed she barely touched her drink, and had a wan sort of appearance.'

'She seemed fearful.'

'It could have been that. Or just that he was bullying her something rotten.'

'And he?'

'Oh, he was full of himself. There was nothing apprehensive about him.'

Gently nodded. 'Then you went in to dinner.'

'Yes. We let them go in first. Then we chose a table in a corner, well away from Mein Herr.' She tapped ash. 'Have you spoken to Bobby?'

'Bobby?'

'Bobby Stratton. The bird man. He was sitting at the next table to them.'

Gently said: 'You are acquainted with Stratton?'

'Known him for yonks,' Miss Cartwright said. 'I used to bank at his bank, and I'm still a member of the bird society. Well, he was there through dinner, though we didn't see him afterwards. He would have to drive back to Wolmering, of course, so he probably left straight after. But if you want impressions of Mein Herr eating his dinner, Bobby is the man to apply to.'

Gently paused, then nodded slowly. 'Carry on,' he said.

'Yes, well,' Miss Cartwright said. 'We finished our meal first, and ordered coffee and liqueurs in the lounge. To start with we had it to ourselves, but then some others filtered in. At last Mein Herr and the mouse came in. They went to sit by the french windows. We did our best to ignore them, and Babs was telling me all about a trip to Normandy she made this summer – she ordered calvados with the coffee, bless her, and it was so strong I nearly choked on it. But we could still hear him droning away, of course, and the mouse putting her little squeaks in. So

122

it was quite a relief – not to mention a surprise – when finally they decided to go out on the patio.'

Gently said: 'When was that?'

'Oh, it must have been getting for ten. There were only them and ourselves left there, and we were beginning to think about leaving.'

'You saw them on the patio?'

'We saw them go out. Of course, you can get that way to the car-park. Anyway, we lit a last fag, and congratulated ourselves on being rid of them.'

'And – then?'

'The mouse came back. Just as we were getting up to go. She let herself in and went straight through the lounge and, I think, into the toilets.'

'You didn't see the man again?'

'No.'

'How long before you left?'

'Perhaps . . . another ten minutes. We ran into Harry – that's the boss – in the hall, and stopped for a few polite words.'

'And the woman didn't reappear?'

'No. For what it's worth, I think she stayed in the toilets. If she'd come out, we must have seen her, and there was no one else about in the hall.' Miss Cartwright stubbed her cigarette out and stared hard at Gently. 'Is that what you wanted?' she said. 'Mein Herr clearing off on his own, to meet that poor fellow down at the quay?'

Gently stared back: there had been something in her voice. She went on scrubbing out the cigarette. At last he said:

'Is it just possible that you were acquainted with Gunther Herschfeldt?'

Miss Cartwright nodded. 'Yes,' she said. 'Molly Hardyment introduced us.'

'Molly . . . Hardyment.'

'Is that so strange?' But now she wasn't looking at

Gently. 'We were pupil teachers together in Shingle-bourne, and I had digs in the town. She introduced me to her people and I spent one Christmas at the farm. It was no surprise to me when I read in the paper that they and Gunther had been celebrating together.'

Gently said: 'Then you knew him well?'

'Not like that!' She made a wry smile. 'Though I couldn't have been blamed. He was a handsome chappie, six feet of gorgeous Teutonic male. But I had other irons in the fire, like a Yankee airman from Idaho. And there were others, I'm very much afraid. Those were heady times for impressionable girls.'

'There would be the airmen from Buxhall.'

'Yes.' She nodded.

'Did Miss Hardyment introduce you to those?'

'She didn't need to. There were plenty around town. One could pick up a Raf boy any evening.'

'Perhaps some you still know?'

'Alas, no.'

Gently said: 'For a while, Robert Stratton was stationed at Buxhall.'

'Was he? Well, I didn't meet him. I'll have to ask about that the next time I see him.'

'He perhaps visited the farm.'

'More than likely.'

'Did Miss Hardyment have any preference for airmen?'

'Well!' She stared for a moment. 'But no doubt you're up to date on all that.'

Gently nodded.

'Yes.' Miss Cartwright pulled a face. 'Of course, she fancied him. We all did. The Land Girl Mabel, me, everyone. But you have to remember he was a POW, someone on the other side of the fence. It wasn't the done thing. It wasn't on. You had to fancy him from a distance. If someone had spotted me chatting him up I would never have been invited to the farm again.'

124

'And yet?' Gently said.

Miss Cartwright sighed. 'I suppose it did happen that way,' she said. 'And yet, to this day, I still can't believe she could have been so crazy. She had other blokes, plenty of them. They were queuing up for Molly. She could have had her pick from half a dozen, and some I'd have given my eye-teeth for. But don't get me wrong, it stopped at first base. To my knowledge it never went further than that. In those days you were either proper or the squadron bike, and Molly certainly wasn't that.'

Gently said: 'You would know most of her conquests.'

'You bet. I shared some of them.'

'She spoke of them to you.'

Miss Cartwright paused. 'There was one I remember her being very cagey about.'

'A serviceman?'

'Weren't they all?'

'Perhaps an airman?'

'Who else? He was very sweet, she told me, a cut above the usual talent. An officer, was my impression. But she always kept him a dead secret.'

'And no name.'

'No.' Miss Cartwright sighed again. 'It was sad, so sad. She was a lovely girl, would have made a splendid teacher. At the time, it really shook me. I was off blokes for quite a while.' She fished out another cigarette. 'Will that be all?' she said.

'All, except for your written statement.'

'Of course,' Miss Cartwright said. 'Of course.'

He left Aspall to superintend the statement and drove the Rover down to the quay. The sun was warm, the tide at slack, and a fishing-boat chugging home up the moorings. He parked where Stratton had parked earlier, got out and stood a moment observing the yacht. Still the curtains

125

were drawn and the cabin door closed, but now a hatch in the roof had been pushed back. He crossed the quay, stepped aboard, and climbed down into the well. At once he heard a soft movement in the cabin, like that of an animal who had been alerted. He tapped on the door.

'Frau Schmeikel?'

'Yes . . . this is who, please?'

Gently announced himself. There was still a long pause before a bolt was shot, and the cabin door eased open. Frau Schmeikel, her hair bedraggled, stared up at him with frightened eyes.

'I am to be arrested . . .yes?'

Gently shook his head. 'May I come in?'

'You do not arrest me?'

'I just wish to talk. About some fresh information that has come in.'

'Fresh . . . information?'

'If you please. But you had better let me come inside.'

She remained staring at him for several moments, but at last backed off down the steps. Gently climbed down after her. The curtained cabin was gloomy, in spite of the hatch pushed back above.

'Shall we pull these curtains?'

'If . . . you wish.'

She crouched on a settee-berth, watching him. The opened curtains admitted the sun and caused her for an instant to cover her eyes. Gently took a seat opposite her. On the cabin table stood an empty cup and a plate on which there were crumbs.

'You have questions for me – yes?'

Gently nodded. 'One or two.'

'It is what Willi has been saying?'

'Not exactly. Our information is from a different source.'

'A different . . .?'

'We have spoken to a lady who also dined at the hotel

on Tuesday. She remembers yourself and your husband. She also took her coffee in the lounge.'

'In the lounge!' Fear was in her staring eyes. 'Of this you have spoken to Willi?'

'Not yet.'

'But you come to me?'

'First, I wish to have your account.'

'But I am telling you everything – everything!'

Gently stared back, and shook his head.

'Oh, this is not fair – not fair!' She covered her face and burst into tears.

Gently shrugged, and sat watching her. Outside, a fishing-boat chugged by. Its wash lifted the *Electra* briefly, pressed her against the tyres that protected her from the quay. Then the yacht settled down again. Trudi Schmeikel dashed at her tears.

'What is she saying then – this lady you speak to?'

'I would sooner have a full account from you.'

'But I have told you!'

'No.'

'It is as I say!'

Gently simply sat silently, shaking his head.

'Oh *Gott, Gott!*' She shed more tears. 'But you will not believe me, yes? And these things you will hold against Willi, whose *Frau* I am. Can this be fair?' She wept. 'So very well. And this is nothing, nothing at all. I am sick, you are understanding? I have had this bug now several days.'

'You are sick . . .?'

'Yes, I am saying. I am as you say, on the run. And it is so at the hotel, when we drink coffee. I am unwell.'

Gently kept staring. 'And so?'

'And so, I feel I must have the air. And we go outside – are you not told so? Because this sickness, I feel it coming on.'

'You and your husband went outside.'

127

'Yes, I say.'

'But only you returned to the hotel.'

'Yes, I am having to, I have the runs badly, I must go back inside.' She wept. 'It is so unfortunate! Now was time to meet Gunther at the quay. Already we are late. I tell Willi, go, and I will be joining you as soon as I can. He is not wanting to, but I insist. It is such bad luck that things happen this way.'

'Very unfortunate,' Gently said. 'And your husband took the garden gate to the street.'

'Yes, is quickest, he goes straight out. No need to go back into the hotel.'

'While you remained.'

'I cannot help this!'

'But in your statement you claim to have accompanied your husband?'

'Yes – no – is true! Very soon I am joining him.' The tears broke out afresh.

Gently said: 'How long did you stay at the hotel?'

She scrubbed her eyes. 'A short time. Very short.'

'Perhaps twenty minutes?'

'No, cannot be! I do not wish to keep them waiting.'

'But longer than ten?'

'I say no. So soon I am following after Willi. I am finding him walking back towards the inn, because there is no Gunther waiting at the quay. He is not there? I say. No, Willi says, he must still be carousing with his peasant friends. But no, he is not at the inn, and they tell us he left them some while since.'

'Did your husband seem concerned?'

'But yes. A little.'

'Perhaps more than a little?'

'Please, do not say that!'

'He was behaving, you would say, quite normally?'

'Yes, yes. Oh, please believe me!'

'And – yet?'

She struggled with her tears. 'You do not know Willi. He is not as you think. He is fond, very fond of his Uncle Gunther. This thing it is impossible he should have done.'

'Was there not some reason why he feared his uncle?'

'No. Never!'

'A matter of finance?'

Her eyes were large. 'You cannot understand! These affairs they are managing together. They are, how you say, realigning the business to take account of the current climate. It is no more.'

'He had nothing to fear?'

'No – no.' But her lips were trembling. Her blue eyes sought Gently's appealingly. 'Please,' she said. 'Please! You must not think such things of him.'

Gently shrugged. Frau Schmeikel hugged herself, hair wet with tears straggling over her face. Outside some other craft puttered by, an outboard dinghy heading for the moorings. She groaned:

'All this – so terrible! And a trip we had planned to be so special. For Uncle Gunther, yes? A celebration. All the summer we are thinking about this trip.'

'To celebrate an anniversary.'

She nodded. 'Is fifty years since he was shot down. He is telling us about it, how it happens, all about those dreadful times in the war.'

'Wasn't he shot down while raiding a local airfield?'

'But yes. You do not know the story?'

'Just a few facts.'

'Then, I must tell you – there can be no secret about it now!' She brushed back the obstructive locks. 'It is the time of the great raids, yes? Night by night, one thousand bombers, attacking first one of our cities, then another. And people die, many people, and the destruction cannot be told. And on one such raid is killed Gunther's mother,

129

also his father is badly hurt. And a pilot is captured who, under interrogation, reveals he came from this airfield here. Do you see?'

Slowly, Gently nodded.

'So. Gunther is a pilot with the Luftwaffe. He is flying Heinkel fighter-bombers in Holland. And he is told this news, and he seeks permission to make revenge raids on this airfield. His family carries weight, he is given permission, and three nights running he attacks this airfield. But your RAF are not so foolish, and on the third night they shoot him down.'

'On . . . 21st October 1944.'

'Yes. Near this same village, here. And the 21st was Tuesday, yes? So we are sailing here to make the celebration.'

'A celebration – with the three of you?'

Trudi Schmeikel hung her head. 'It could not be helped! Gunther met these people, and Willi – you know? You cannot change a man, what he is. At first, we are all going to the hotel, that is how we have planned. But then there were these people, and Gunther chose the inn instead.'

'It was all quite amicable.'

'Oh yes. Gunther knew Willi. He did not mind. I am thinking perhaps he is wanting it this way, to have the peasant people on his own.'

'It was just . . . unfortunate.'

'Yes.' But Trudi Schmeikel didn't catch his eye.

Gently said: 'Till then, a pleasant trip?'

Now she looked at him. 'I think so, yes.'

'No problems, apart from running into those people?'

She shook her head, then hesitated. 'Oh yes. Is one small thing.'

'What was that?'

'I do not know, but Gunther said a man tried to rob him. He is after his camera, he thinks, but Gunther quickly chases him away. It is at the reserve, on Sunday, when he goes to photograph that bird.'

'At the reserve . . . did he describe him?'

'Only that he is old enough to know better. But perhaps it was nothing at all, and Gunther does not understand this man.'

Gently thought about it, then shrugged. 'And there have been no other incidents while you were here?'

'No, I do not think so. Everywhere people have been pleasant to us.'

'The problem with your mooring-buoy?'

'Oh, is nothing! Willi took care of that foolish man.' She paused, her eyes seeking Gently's. 'Willi – he is still to be kept locked up?'

'I'm afraid so.'

'But . . .!' Her eyes fell again. 'At least, perhaps, I may see him?'

'Perhaps this evening.'

'But not now?'

'Our investigation is still in progress, Frau Schmeikel.'

'But just to see him!'

'I'm truly sorry.'

Trudi Schmeikel flung away from him. 'Willi is innocent!' she exclaimed. 'He would not do this thing to his uncle. He is innocent, an innocent man. Can you not tell that?'

Gently stared for a long moment. He said: 'And can you?'

'Yes. Yes, yes!'

But then Frau Schmeikel collapsed again in a passion of tears.

It seemed inevitable that, when he climbed back on the quay, the first thing his eye lit on was the blue Corsa,

131

parked at no great distance from the Rover, and with
Stratton lounging beside it. The ex-bank man had glasses
in his hand, and was gazing down the moorings at some
swimming wildfowl. But seeing Gently, he lowered the
glasses and came forward with an ingratiating smile.

'You wished to speak to me?'

Stratton seemed uncertain. He fiddled with the focus
on the glasses. 'It's nothing, really! I just wanted to say
again how sorry I was.'

'How sorry?'

'Yes. I was a bit abrupt with you. I suppose I'm not
used to this sort of thing. But I didn't want to leave you
with a wrong impression – I mean, we're neighbours,
know some of the same people.' He smiled awkwardly. 'I
rang Andy Reymerston. He seems to be a great admirer
of yours. He told me in no uncertain terms that you were
a man I could put my trust in.'

Gently shrugged. 'Then you have something to tell
me?'

'Well – no! Not exactly that. Only to apologise again if I
seemed surly and less than co-operative.'

Gently shrugged again. He looked down the moorings
to where the wildfowl still swam in a group. He said:

'Perhaps I can help you. Is that Little Egret still present
at Grimchurch reserve?'

'The Little Egret . . .?'

'Yes. Is it still in the pool to which you were directing
Herschfeldt on Sunday?'

There was no smile in Stratton's eyes now. He turned
his face away and stared at the Corsa. Finally he said, not
looking at Gently: 'Then someone has told you about
that?'

'We have our sources.'

'Someone saw . . .?'

'A person of your description was mentioned.'

132

'Oh lord!' Now Stratton turned. 'But what did they say? What did they tell you?'

Gently said: 'The incident was reported. Herschfeldt spoke of being attacked. He supposed the object was the theft of his camera. He alleged that he resisted and that his assailant fled.'

'And you think that I . . .!'

'Were you that man, Stratton?'

'Oh lord!' Stratton gaped. 'But it . . . it all happened the other way round!'

'The other way?'

'Yes. I wasn't the attacker. And I certainly wasn't trying to steal his camera!'

Gently stared hard into the scared grey eyes. 'Perhaps you had better explain,' he said.

'Yes, explain,' Stratton gabbled. 'Oh dear. I know I should have mentioned this to you before.' He turned to stare at the Corsa again. He said: 'I took him down to the stream, you know? Down the slope to the track along the bank, where it is concealed by alders and willows. I was prepared to go the whole way with him, in case he got side-tracked further along. He seemed quite friendly when we started, chatting about the birds that were coming in, and then, I don't know, he became silent, seemed almost to resent my being with him. And when we got among the trees, suddenly he turned on me. Believe it or not, he accused me of spying on him!'

'Of . . . spying on him?'

'Yes. It was unbelievable! And then he began shoving me away down the track. And just then some other people came along, so I simply turned my back and left him to it.' Stratton faced Gently with an indignant stare. 'I still can't think what it was all about!'

Gently stared back. 'As you say. Unbelievable.'

'And now, it seems, he accused me of trying to steal his

133

camera! It may be after all he was a man with a secret, and that had something to do with what happened here.'

Gently said: 'And this you didn't think to tell me?'

'Well . . . the man was dead. I couldn't see the point.'

'And still you tell me you didn't recognise him later – when you and he were alone together on this quay?'

'No. I simply didn't!'

'In the full glare of your headlights?'

'I told you – I wasn't looking his way! And if I'd seen who it was I would have left sooner. I certainly didn't want to run into him again.'

Gently shook his head.

'You believe me, don't you?'

Gently said: 'I've heard stranger stories before.'

'But – can you imagine me trying to steal his camera?'

'Perhaps not that,' Gently said.

'Then . . .?'

Gently shrugged. 'You spoke of co-operation,' he said. 'Perhaps on another point you can be helpful. I'm still trying to get a picture of what happened during the war. How long were you stationed at RAF Buxhall?'

At once Stratton froze. 'That . . . has nothing to do with it!'

'You were there at the time of the raids, weren't you?'

'I've told you all I can about that. I was at home on leave when they happened.'

'What was your position at Buxhall?'

Stratton almost spat it. 'I was an admin officer.'

'You had rank?'

'A Flight-Lieuy. And I finished up Squadron Leader.'

'And . . . at that time . . . life wasn't all business? One got out of camp now and then?'

'So if one did?'

'There'd be flicks, dances, a social life going on outside?'

'Look, I told you – !' Stratton began, then halted. 'I'm sorry,' he said. 'But I must be getting home. I've told you all I can. If you need me again, I shall be at home all the evening.'

Gently said: 'In those days, would you have known Miss Jessica Cartwright?'

'No I wouldn't. And now I must go!'

'Or an attractive friend of hers?'

He shook his head. And bolted.

Gently watched him cram into the Corsa and drive jerkily away over the flood-ramp; then turned back to look at the *Electra*, across whose cabin windows the curtains were once more drawn.

At just that moment, Shavers appeared, as though to complete the prospectus. But Gently got into the Rover and drove off after Stratton.

9

'Look, Gently, do me a favour, and get their damned Embassy off my back! Every five minutes my phone is ringing and they're demanding to know why we haven't charged Schmeikel. It was bad enough before he tried to skip, but now they seem nervous as kittens. One gets the impression that, unless we fix him, the Bundesbank and all will be up the spout.'

Back in the office Gently had rung Reymerston, who had sounded concerned about his interest in Stratton; and he had scarcely laid down the phone when an irascible AC was on the other end.

'How close are we now, confound it? Surely this attempt to bolt must swing it? I tell you, Gently, if there's half a case there I want some action, and I want it today. Well?'

'The case is nearly complete . . .'

'Today, Gently. Not tomorrow!'

'Just minor matters to clear up.'

'Then get your finger out, and damn well clear them!'

Yet . . . were those matters so minor? Gently hung up and remained staring at the phone. Reymerston, at least, had no doubts about Stratton – an eccentric, perhaps, but basically a sound egg.

'Old lad, you can keep your eagle eye off Bobby! There's no one in Suffolk less likely to bash a Kraut. We've known him for fifteen years at least, and there isn't a gentler character on God's earth.'

'Would you have met his wife?'

'Don't think he ever had one – anyway, not since we've known him. You get the impression he's one of nature's bachelors, just married to his birds and all that. He has an apartment on the front at Wolmering – I've been there, he keeps it like a new pin. When he comes here, he always brings a bottle with him, and sometimes a posy of flowers for Ruth.'

'Does he ever talk about himself?'

'No. He admires my daubs, and Ruth's garden. For the rest, it's the birds, what's coming, what's going, and whether I prefer Roland Green to Peter Scott.'

'No mention of his wartime exploits.'

'Didn't know he'd ever had any!'

'He was in the RAF. For a while at Buxhall.'

'Well, it's never been a subject of conversation. He sometimes talks about the bank, and I got the impression he'd spent his whole life in it. But of course, at his age, he must have done service. Don't tell me he's one of our unsung heroes.'

'Just an admin officer.'

'Yes . . . that follows! So probably he had a quiet war. But why are you asking?'

Gently shrugged to himself. 'Just filling in the picture!'

'But what picture, old lad?'

'Stratton is a witness.'

There was a pause at Reymerston's end. 'Well, as long as that's all,' he said. 'You can surely depend on him for that. But for heaven's sake don't start getting other ideas, not about our Bobby. Just stay with the Kraut.'

Which advice was immediately repeated with greater unction by the AC . . .

Aspall had been in on the latter conversation, and had

137

listened solemnly to Gently's responses. When the phone was hung up, he ventured:

'But we really can't need so much more now, sir!'

'You mean – now we've got Schmeikel alone on the quay?'

'That's what we've been after, sir, all along. His wife lied, but she's been caught out. And now we've got Schmeikel where we want him.'

Gently said: 'I think Frau Schmeikel was probably telling me the truth.'

'Can't see it matters either way, sir.'

'It would mean that what happened on the quay wasn't planned, but suddenly blew up, and was over in minutes.'

'Could have been like that, sir.'

Gently shook his head. 'It has to leave an element of doubt. There was no time for a dispute to develop to the point of homicidal violence.'

'So then he just took his opportunity, sir.'

'That is the way we would be obliged to present it.'

'Well, it suits me, sir!'

'It still weakens the case.'

Aspall shrugged, and gave Gently a shrewd look. 'Are we still thinking of Stratton, sir?' he said.

'Of Stratton.' Gently nodded. 'And what happened at Grimchurch reserve.'

Aspall made a face. 'Well, I don't know, sir. There might just have been something going on there. But I can't see it upsetting our case, not with everything we've got on Schmeikel.'

'Stratton is our principal witness.'

'Even so, sir.'

'We can't afford to have him discredited.'

'Well . . . if you say so, sir.' But Aspall looked as though he thought this was splitting hairs.

Gently checked his watch. He said: 'I think we can make Grange Farm in time for tea. It may be that they remember Miss Jessica Cartwright, and perhaps a little more of the affairs of those days.'

'You mean – Stratton and that suicide girl, sir?'

'If there's a link, we have to have it,' Gently said.

Sighing, Aspall got to his feet. 'At least that Mabs woman knows how to cook!' he said.

Symbolically, it seemed, a pair of the ground-assault aircraft skimmed across the landscape ahead of them, and disappeared behind trees as they approached the lane leading to the farm.

Was the airfield two miles, three miles away? It was handy for Thwaite, the nearest village, which boasted three separate pubs, and no more than fifteen minutes' drive from the town of Shinglebourne for airmen equipped with transport. And in Shinglebourne there was a cinema, a dance-hall, hotels, in wartime probably a servicemen's club. From Buxhall the off-duty personnel would flock there to drink, dance and sample the local talent. Airmen. Officers. A good-looking young Flight-Lieuy – was it possible that Stratton hadn't joined in with the others? Hadn't picked up his quota of girls, including always that one more special than the rest? And so perhaps it had flourished, that wartime romance, promises, vows had been exchanged, dreams dreamed, plans made, a future seen beckoning from 'after the war'. Only then he had been posted, the young Flight-Lieuy, first to the next county, afterwards to France; and the letters, strangely, they had stopped coming, never again was there one addressed in that special handwriting. What could have happened? For long months, he didn't know. And then, on his first leave, he'd have hastened back to the small town, there to learn – it was current gossip – in what way his dream had died. His first dream, his last dream. Never again was his heart to be given. He returned to the bank and his bachelor living, and the birds that replaced the love torn from his heart . . .

Wasn't that the scenario, the drama behind the next fifty solitary years, a tragic potential, passive, waiting, ready to be jolted into violent action? The roar of the two aircraft seemed to embody it, to close the gap of those empty years.

As usual, the approach of the car had alerted old Willum, who was waiting in the porch to welcome them. He hobbled down the steps as Gently parked and came round to open the car door.

'You boys have learnt when to turn up here – our Mabs is getting the shortcakes out now!' He chuckled. 'Do you like them hot? Blast, they go down a treat with a swig of tea.'

He ushered them in. The house was warm and redolent with the smell of baking. From the kitchen came the sounds of utensils being manoeuvred and the voices of Mabs and Cynthy. In the dining-room Jimmy sat alone with his paper, but there was no sign of Nellie or his son. As they entered Jimmy set his paper aside and rose to acknowledge the newcomers.

'See you caught the bugger, then – it's in the stop-press in the *Evening*! Give you any trouble, did he?'

Gently shook his head and took a chair.

'I'd like to have been there,' Jimmy said. 'I'd like to have given you a hand with the sod. You can tell with some blokes. He was one. You could see it as soon as you clapped eyes on him.' He paused. 'Admitted it, has he?'

'You watch your tongue, Jimmy!' Willum said. 'You mustn't go asking him things like that, just because he drops in for a cup of tea.'

'He hasn't just dropped in,' Jimmy said. 'Not him.'

'Well, you wait till he's had his tea.'

'After something, he is.'

140

'Jimmy,' Willum said.

'Only asking,' Jimmy said. 'Only asking.'

And fifty years since, had it been much different – the ready hospitality, the smell of baking? When Jimmy had been just a kid, and Willum a man at the height of his powers? It was a house that exuded friendship, and in the war they were better off than most to extend it – rationing would barely have touched Grange Farm, and where it did they'd have goods to barter. Take this chicken, this dozen eggs back with you . . . wouldn't have some sugar going spare, would you? Friends were invited there freely: Jessica Cartwright for all of Christmas . . .

The hatch slid back, and Mabs counted heads. Then the tea-tray arrived and a dish piled with shortcakes. Mabs poured while Cynthy served the cakes – hot, sweet, melting pastry studded with currants. It seemed the very flavour of Grange Farm, and to come back for more an act of politeness. They ate and drank. Mabs said:

'You'll be finished here, will you? Got it all sorted out?'

Gently said: 'Just a few details. We like to fill in the picture.' He took his second shortcake. He said: 'I've been talking to a lady called Jessica Cartwright. She said she knew you a long time back, spent a Christmas here when she was a girl.'

'Jessy?' Mabs stared. 'I didn't know she was still around.'

'She's retired, of course. She used to teach at Hunting-field. Now she's living in a cottage at Thwaite.'

'Jessy Cartwright?'

Gently nodded.

'I remember her,' Jimmy said. 'I thought she was the goods. Molly brought her back here.' He smirked. 'Mabs was jealous. I was courting her, then.'

'And I was just their Land Girl,' Mabs snorted. 'While Lady Jessy was training to be a teacher. But I don't care. It was me he married, and he can't get away from that.'

Gently said: 'She was friendly with Molly. They used to go about a great deal together. They seemed to have shared all their boyfriends but one, and that one Molly always kept a secret. You wouldn't know who he was?'

Mabs looked at Jimmy, and Jimmy at Mabs. 'She always had plenty,' Mabs said. 'I don't want to speak ill of her now, but everyone will tell you. She was like that.'

'An RAF man, Miss Cartwright thought.'

'Several of those,' Mabs said.

'He may have been an officer.'

'Sounds like Molly.'

'Possibly one who was stationed at Buxhall.'

Mabs shook her head. 'She brought a few of them home here. I remember a Flight-Sergeant air-gunner. But no officers, not RAF. There was only that Army fellow with the car.'

'A tall fellow he might have been. Rather good-looking.'

But Mabs only went on shaking her head. 'Perhaps he was married, and then she would have kept it dark. Things weren't the same in those days as they are now.'

Gently said: 'Did she receive many letters?'

'Oh, plenty of those,' Mabs said. 'I saw some of them. They were a giggle. You wouldn't believe what some blokes wrote.'

'Did she keep many of them?'

'Shouldn't think so.'

'You can't bring any names to mind?'

She thought about it. 'One was called Colin. I remember him because he wrote some verse. Then there was one she called Ozzie, but I never knew what his real name was.'

'For example, no Roberts.'

'May have been. But none I can bring to mind.'

Gently said: 'And of course, none of those letters now exist?'

'No. They'd have been slung out years ago.'

'Hold you hard!' Willum broke in. 'Hold you hard.' He turned a misty eye on Gently. 'You got a reason for this, old partner?' he said. 'This isn't just along of curiosity?'

'Not quite,' Gently said.

'Ah, I'm thinking.' Willum's gaze dropped to his cup. 'All this about poor little Molly, you wouldn't be bringing it up for nothing.' He touched his eye. 'Men liked her,' he said. 'And she wasn't to blame for that. She was a pretty one, a right pretty gal, the dead spit of her mother when she was that age.' He hesitated. 'So what are you on about? Who is this man you say she took up with?'

Gently said: 'We need to identify him. He may have been involved in what happened on Tuesday.'

'And you don't know who he is?'

'We may have an idea.'

'Seems a rummun to me,' Willum said. 'But there you are, it's your business, and you're a bloke who knows what's what.'

Gently said nothing.

'Them letters,' Willum said. He sniffed hard. 'Stuck them away with the rest of her things,' he said. 'Her mother couldn't bear to see them, nor I couldn't bear to chuck them away. I shoved them in a chest up in the loft. Though I daresay the moths have got them by now. But that's where you'll find them, up there. In the old chest shoved behind the tank.'

'So that's what's in that chest!' Mabs exclaimed. 'I've often wondered when I've been up there.'

'Her clothes, her little bits,' Willum said. He jammed his lips tight shut, kept staring at the cup.

Mabs looked at Gently.

'I'm sorry,' Gently said. 'But I have to ask if I may see those letters. I don't need to read them. All we require is to discover the identity of the writer.'

'Better get them,' Willum said. 'Take him up there.'

'Oh dear!' Mabs jumped up and put her arm round Willum.

'No – don't you, don't you!' He pushed her away. 'You'll have me snivelling, and we don't want that. Just take him up there, gal. And see you put the things back afterwards.'

'I suppose I'll have to.'

'Ah,' Willum said. 'And you can pour me another cup first.'

Mabs hastened to pour him one. Then she gestured to Gently. Gently followed her out of the room. She led him upstairs to a gloomy landing and along it to a trapdoor in the ceiling.

'There's a ladder inside . . .'

She found him a chair, and standing on it he pushed back the door and pulled down the loft-ladder. He let Mabs mount first. Up there was complete darkness. Mabs fumbled for a switch. A single bulb, without a shade, dimly lit the loft and the collection of ages. Dust lay heavy, and spiders' webs, and a smell of decay was in the air.

'The tank's down here . . .'

The light barely reached it, or the old cloth-covered travelling-chest thrust in behind it. Dust rose as Gently bent to prise it out and generations of spiders' webs were left trailing.

'Better bring it this way . . .'

He lugged it down to the light. Webbing straps and buckles were all that secured it. He lugged them apart and raised the lid, releasing an odour of damp and dissolution.

'Oh my God!'

Mabs fumbled in the chest. Fabric parted as she drew out a dress. Garments, barely recognisable, stuck together, tore as she sought to pull them apart. An ebony box contained a few trinkets, and a watch that had stopped fifty years ago. A pair of high-heeled shoes were green with mould, a felt hat holed by moths. Then there was a package tied with a stained, faded ribbon.

'Here . . .'

Gently took the package. The ribbon crumbled as he attemped to undo it, the bundle of letters came apart in his hands. He unfolded one and held it to the light. It was dated 6th June 1944, and addressed from the Officers' Mess, RAF Buxhall. It began: 'Dearest Girl'. Gently read no further. He turned to the signature at the end. After a suitably flowery conclusion, underlined with a flourish, appeared the name: Osbert.

Hastily he sampled a fresh letter, but the handwriting, the name were the same. Every letter had come from the same man, and he caught a plaintive phrase or two occurring in the later ones. 'Impatient Girl' was the final mode of address: the last letter was dated 10th May 1945.

'Are there any others?'

'I don't think so.'

Mabs felt around in the damp lining of the chest. Then, in one of the side-pockets, she came up with a yellowed snapshot. Gently took it. On the back was scrawled: 'All my love – for always', in the same handwriting as the letters, and the photograph was of a smiling man in RAF battledress.

He stared long at the faded photograph – fifty years had intervened! But then he handed the snapshot back to Mabs. Molly's lover had worn wings. He had been a pilot.

'Did you find what you wanted, old partner?'

Somehow, old Willum had got the better of his distress. With an empty cup before him, and a crumby plate, he sat puffing at his clay pipe. Jimmy also had his pipe going, and Cynthy was collecting the tea-things on a tray. Aspall

145

sat looking bored. He threw Gently a questioning look as he entered.

'Yes, thank you.'

'And was he your bloke, then?'

Aspall was also wanting to know that! Gently took his seat again. 'We may have made some progress,' he said.

'Ah,' Willum said. 'So like that he wasn't.'

'All information can be helpful.'

'But he wasn't him you thought.'

Gently shrugged, got out his pipe and joined the smokers. He let a few puffs go by. He said:

'Did you get a good look at that bird on Sunday?'

'Oh ah,' Willum said. 'Wasn't going to miss the likes of him.'

'You've always been keen on birds.'

'Since I was a nipper,' Willum said. 'Jimmy, he don't take after me in that, nor yet Nellie. But Markie's keen.'

'You'll be a member of the local society.'

'Ah.'

'So you'll perhaps know Mr Stratton.'

'We all know him,' Mabs said. 'We knew him at the bank a long time ago.' She sniffed. 'He's barmier than Willum about birds.'

'He's all right,' Jimmy said. 'Just a bit quaint. He lives on his own.'

'Not surprising,' Mabs sniffed. 'Who'd have him?'

'Oh, go on,' Jimmy said.

Gently said: 'Did you see him at the reserve on Sunday?'

'I saw him,' Mabs said. 'I don't know about the others. He was up at The Pulk when we were there, and then afterwards at the caff.'

'You saw him in the coffee room?'

'Two tables away.'

'Ah yes, I remember now!' Jimmy said. 'But it was when old Gunther was with us, we weren't paying much attention to anyone else.'

146

'You should have been there, boy,' Willum said. He shook his head. 'It's all such a shame. No one could have guessed, when we were yarning there, that things were going to finish up like this.'

'They should string that nephew up,' Mabs said. 'I would, if it was up to me.'

'Makes you feel like it,' Jimmy said.

Willum shook his head afresh.

Gently drew on his pipe. He said: 'And this was the first time you heard where your friend had been shot down.'

'The first time,' Willum said. 'We never knew, back there in '45. Told us he was shot down on a raid, like, but that's as far as he went. Daresay he thought we would hold it against him, I don't know. But he never said.'

'He told you of the raids.'

'Ah. But they weren't any concern of ours.'

'Three raids on the trot?'

'No doubt he had orders. You did what you were told in them days, boy.'

'And then . . . his shooting down at Harford.'

'Ah.' Willum's misty eyes sparkled. 'Why he come over here, wasn't it, for a bit of a knees-up down there.'

'Fifty years later.'

'Fifty-odd year. He could even remember the weather that day. A full moon, he says, with a frost, and him dangling there up that tree. Says he'll never forget that. He could see the church and the castle quite plain. When he got back home he looked it up on a map, and that's how he knew where the place was.'

'And Tuesday would be the fiftieth anniversary.'

Willum puffed. 'Nor we shan't forget it. A rare old evening. And then, to think . . .' He shook his head.

Gently said: 'Was it he who suggested you meet him there?'

'Ah. Asked if we knew a good pub near the waterfront.

147

Told him the Mariners, and that's what we settled on. I knew we'd be all right there.'

'So everything was arranged. There in the coffee room.'

'He come out with us afterwards,' Willum said. 'Saw us to the cars. Like he did on Tuesday. Shook every last one by the hand.'

'Was his nephew with him then?'

'No he wasn't! We never saw no more of him.'

'When you drove away, you left him there alone.'

Willum lowered his head. 'Like on Tuesday,' he said.

Gently drew on a dead pipe. 'Some time after that your friend appears to have run into Mr Stratton. Mr Stratton was present in the coffee room with you. I suppose you wouldn't have introduced them?'

'Didn't know he was there,' Willum said. 'Mabs may have seen him. I didn't.'

'Can't think why we'd introduce them,' Mabs said. 'Mr Stratton is no great pal of ours.'

'You wouldn't have met him in the old days.'

Mabs stared. 'So when would they be?'

'During the war he was stationed at Buxhall.'

She shook her head. 'We never ran across him.'

Gently glanced at the others. 'None of you?'

'Don't look at me!' Jimmy said.

'I wasn't born,' Cynthy said.

'Never knew he was at Buxhall,' Willum said. He screwed his eyes up. 'Seems to me you're rare interested in the man,' he said.

Gently ignored him. He said: 'Perhaps, in the coffee room, Mr Stratton overheard some of the conversation. When they met later he went out of his way to show your friend where he would find the egret.'

'Could have been listening,' Mabs said. 'Though he seemed to be staring out of the window. But he got up and went out before we did. I can't remember if I saw him outside.'

148

'He left just before you did.'

'Yes, he did. So he'd be somewhere about there.'

'No doubt he would wait till you left before introducing himself.'

Mabs sniffed. 'If you say so.'

Willum's eyes were screwed up yet tighter. 'So do he come into it, boy?' he said. 'With you one never can't tell. It's like all this squit about poor little Molly.'

Gently sank his head. 'My apologies again.'

'But do he come into it?'

'He's part of the picture.'

'And that's all you're going to tell us,' Willum said. 'Ah well, no doubt it'll come out one day.' He sighed.

'More tea?' Mabs said. 'We'll need another pot when Nellie comes in.'

Gently shook his head, and rose.

'You come again, boy,' Willum said. 'Any time. We're always here.'

Aspall was silent while they drove down the lane and made the turn into the back road. Then he gave Gently a cautious little glance. 'Well – I reckon that's that, sir!' he said.

Gently drove. He said: 'Stratton was lying. He knew from the first who Herschfeldt was.'

'But he wasn't the bloke, sir. The one who wrote the letters. Seems there's no connection between him and what happened back there.'

'Then why did he lie?'

Aspall wriggled his shoulders. 'Perhaps he never heard that talk in the coffee room! We don't know he did, and no one can prove it. And even if he did, well there you are.'

'I think he must have heard it.'

'So what if he did, sir?'

'He knew where to look for Herschfeldt on Tuesday.'

'But that might be why he lied, sir. He found himself in a spot. He was down at the quay when Herschfeldt bought it.'

'By – pure coincidence?'

'Could have been, sir. Or maybe he was curious, knowing what was going on there. And now we've dug around, and can't find any sort of connection, I reckon we just have to accept him as an Honest John witness.' Aspall stared ahead determinedly. 'I'm happy with him, sir. And you have to remember he volunteered. If he hadn't, we might never have found him.'

Gently drove. 'And that encounter on Sunday?'

'He's given us his account, sir. It could have happened like he said.'

'A somewhat questionable account!'

'No more than what Herschfeldt told the woman, sir. It was probably the way she said, just a silly misunderstanding.'

'So . . . we give Stratton a clean bill.'

'Near enough, sir. I reckon we've got him out of the way. And now we can go ahead with Schmeikel and see how he stands up when he hears what we've got.'

Gently shrugged. 'The last nail!'

'He's the one who's got to explain a lie, sir.'

The sun was setting, the mist rising again as they crossed the square and drew up at the police station. Slatter must have seen them arrive, since he came out of the office to meet them.

'I've had the Jerries on the line, sir, the German Embassy. They wanted to make sure we were holding Schmeikel here. They're sending a couple of their blokes down to interview him, said we could expect them any time soon.'

'Did they say what it was about?'

'No sir. Just said to regard it as urgent. They gave me

150

the names of the blokes who're coming – I wrote them down. A Herr Stern and a Herr Reinbeck.'

'Oh damn!' Aspall said. 'Do we have to hang on, sir?'

'We'll have to give them their turn,' Gently said.

'But we could be wrapping this business up!'

'I'm afraid we must remember that he is their national.'

'They did say it was urgent, sir,' Slatter said.

Aspall swore again. But there was nothing for it. They sat down to wait in the glooming office. Coffee came and went, and Gently smoked two pipes before a black Mercedes limousine emerged into the square. Slatter was sent to marshal it in. He returned leading two gentlemen in city suits, one of them clasping a fat brief-case.

'Herr Gently, please?'

Gently rose.

'I am Herr Stern, First Secretary of our Embassy. And here is Herr Reinbeck, our legal attaché, who brings with him the documents concerning the case.'

'The – documents?'

Herr Stern nodded briskly. 'This affair runs deeper than perhaps you are told. Let us say that what has happened here is no great surprise to those familiar with the facts. May I sit down?'

'Please do,' Gently said. Aspall rose hastily to supply an extra chair. Herr Stern and Herr Reinbeck sat themselves down, the latter depositing his brief-case on the desk.

Outside, a uniformed chauffeur stood almost to attention by the black limousine.

10

'May I enquire if Wilhelm Schmeikel has yet been charged with the death of his uncle?'

Herr Stern was a full-bodied gentleman with plump features and a shock of unexpectedly brown hair. In his mid-fifties, he had a growling voice, and a habit of tilting his chin when he spoke. His companion was perhaps a year or two younger, of slighter build, with hawkish features.

'The case against him is very strong.'

'Ah. You are perhaps awaiting certain additional information. Such information we have brought. It will doubtless enable you to proceed. In return, my colleague and I will wish to interview this man. It is understood?'

'Understood.'

Herr Stern leaned a little closer. 'Some information has, I believe, already been divulged, concerning the alleged misbehaviour of Wilhelm Schmeikel?'

Gently nodded. 'Concerning matters of finance.'

Herr Stern tossed his head. 'My dear friend! We are not now speaking of petty defalcations, but of such tangled machinations as may embarrass governments. Doubtless you will recall the case of Robert Maxwell?'

'Maxwell . . .?'

'But yes. And does not that then raise parallels? He, too, disappeared from his yacht, and in circumstances that remain mysterious.' Herr Stern fixed Gently's eye.

'This is the surprise, that Gunther Herschfeldt did not disappear sooner – say, at sea, with no witness, no English police to ask awkward questions. Why is Schmeikel waiting so long, hah? Can it be the presence of his wife that prevents him? And so, on Tuesday, occurs the opportunity, yes – your enquiry succeeds in revealing this?'

Gently stared silently. Then nodded.

'So, that is the answer,' Herr Stern growled. 'He waits till a witness so awkward is absent, and then this accident takes place. Is a circumstance, but no witness. From your case, this still is missing. A motive you require, a motive overwhelming.' He pointed to the brief-case. 'This.'

Gently eyed the brief-case. He said: 'Perhaps you will explain?'

Herr Stern sat back. 'Is involved,' he said. 'Is complicated. First, you must understand that Herschfeldt Electronics is a major player in the field. It has absorbed this company and that. It owns firms through Europe and in America. Its cash value runs to many billions and in Germany it is one of the largest employers. Thus its stability is of major importance, and the Bundesbank also is deeply involved. But, sadly, the demand for its products is wavering, there is over-supply, both at home and abroad. I make the situation plain?'

Gently nodded assent.

'So, there is the problem. And what is Herschfeldt's answer? Diversification. He will sell, he will withdraw capital, he will reinvest in industries more profitable. Oh yes, it is prudent, it is sensible, it is the strategy of successful entrepreneurs. Some part of this plan is already carried out, and a few token investments made.'

'Token investments . . .?'

Herr Stern looked at Herr Reinbeck. Herr Reinbeck said: 'The figures are an estimate. Perhaps five per cent of the capital realised, but the exact figure of the latter is not available.'

Herr Stern nodded ponderously. 'And there you have it, my friend. Five per cent only of that capital invested. And the balance untraceable. A balance that includes the liquidated funds of two pension schemes. An informed estimate quotes seven billion marks as missing from the accounts of Herschfeldt Electronics.'

Gently stared. 'And for this you hold Schmeikel responsible?'

Herr Stern extended a plump hand. 'He and his uncle. Both. We have documents flown in this morning. They show Schmeikel as the instrument by which the funds were transferred. The funds are in Switzerland, this we know, but it is Schmeikel who holds the key. Thus, he had but to get rid of his uncle, and this, as you know, he achieved.'

'He killed him for the money?'

'What else? And what further can you need to complete your case?'

'You can prove he is in sole possession of those funds?'

'The documentation can scarcely be denied.' Herr Stern eased back again in his seat. 'Now we wish to face him with this,' he said. 'If he is sensible he will assist us to recover those funds again. It can do him no harm, and perhaps good, it may enable his defence to mount a plea for clemency. His years in your prison may be less. This consideration my colleague will put to him. It is agreed?'

Gently paused before nodding. He glanced at Aspall. Aspall rose and left. Herr Stern folded his hands with satisfaction. He said:

'Tonight we shall wrap this up, yes?'

Gently yielded his chair at the desk and placed another before it for Schmeikel. Herr Reinbeck also drew close to the desk, where he unbuckled the fat brief-case. Files, read-outs and forms came out of it, accompanied by a

154

bunch of faxes. Herr Reinbeck laid them out tidily and placed the brief-case beside his chair. Then Aspall returned, shepherding Schmeikel. Schmeikel halted, staring, when he saw the set-up. But Aspall guided him to the chair and firmly assisted him to sit. Schmeikel stared at Herr Stern with large eyes. Herr Stern let his gaze wander over Schmeikel.

'*Sie sind Wilhelm Schmeikel?*'

'*Ja.*'

Agreeably, Herr Stern introduced himself and his colleague. There followed what sounded like an almost light-hearted few words of explanation. Herr Stern waved his hand. His eye was lively. One half expected to catch him smiling. Then his little speech ended in an appealing peroration, with the hand held out towards Schmeikel. Schmeikel shrank from him.

'*Nein!*'

'*Was – nein?*'

'*Ich sagt nein!*'

'*Aber, mein gut freund . . .!*'

Herr Stern began again, his tone this time more solemn. It got him nowhere. Schmeikel went on staring at him with hostile eyes, and, at the peroration, once more snapped:

'*Nein!*'

'*Ach!*' Herr stern waved to Herr Reinbeck. '*Sprechen Sie zu ihm, Franz.*'

Herr Reinbeck cleared his throat. His manner of approach was more measured. He peeled a fax from the bunch and exhibited it for Schmeikel to read. He held forth in precise terms. He used his finger to make points. Finally he unfurled a lengthy read-out and spread it out over the desk. Schmeikel glared at it with angry eyes.

'*Ist lügen – alle lügen!*'

'*Sie mich verstehen, Schmeikel?*'

'*Ja – und Ich sagt nein!*'

Patiently, expressionlessly, Herr Reinbeck resumed his

discourse. His finger ran down the read-out. He quoted figures, peeled off a fresh fax. On his chair Schmeikel sat bolt upright, his expression ever more savage. His fists were clenching and unclenching. At last he hissed the word:

'*Kot!*'

Herr Stern gazed at him. He said another word. Schmeikel came back with several more. They glared at each other, and Schmeikel tried to jump up, but the alert Aspall assisted him to sit again. Herr Stern hurled fresh words. Herr Reinbeck made a restraining gesture. Then Schmeikel began to storm at Herr Stern, stretching forward, waving his fists. He carried on. He wouldn't be stopped. The sweat stood out on his wrinkled brow. His uncle's name was spoken frequently, and there were references to *Die Schweiz*. He pounded on the desk to make his points. He thrust savage fingers at Herr Reinbeck and his documents. Finally, when he ran out of breath, Herr Stern snapped a contemptuous question. And then it all began again, with Herr Stern seizing on every interval. Minutes passed, quarter of an hour, and still the snarling exchange continued.

Eventually, Herr Reinbeck began to gather up the papers and stow them away again in his brief-case. That done, he laid the brief-case on the desk, adjusting it to sit quite square. Then he murmured a quiet word, at the same time glancing at his watch. For a moment it seemed Herr Stern would ignore him. But then he threw up his hands in a gesture of resignation.

'Take him away, this criminal! I am ashamed to own him as a fellow countryman.'

Gently said: 'You have finished with him?'

'I have finished. He belongs to you!'

Aspall touched Schmeikel's shoulder. Schmeikel sprang up, still glaring at Herr Stern. In German, he hurled some final insult, then allowed himself to be led out. Herr Stern wiped his brow.

'No use,' he said. 'No use! That dog is doomed. He spurns our assistance. His trial I shall watch with the greatest interest.'

Gently said: 'He denies your allegations?'

'On every count he denies them. I am slandering him, he says, and his Uncle Gunther, they are honest people, they commit no offence.'

'In the case of the pension funds?'

'Even there! He swears it is all done with the best intention. Because of the recession, the falling dividends, they propose to reinvest the funds in bonds.'

Gently paused. 'Would that be credible?'

Herr Reinbeck said: 'As a short or medium-term strategy, yes. But one would expect a balance of bonds and equities, which is not the case here.'

'Yet it could be represented as a proper undertaking?'

'If the bonds had been purchased, I agree.'

'Which – is not the case?'

'No. The funds have vanished, as you say, into the blue.'

'*Ach!*' Herr Stern exclaimed. 'Do not waste your time trying to defend him. If it were honest he would tell us where these missing funds might be recovered. But no. He blankly refuses. I am told it is the business of his firm, and no other. Herr Gently, you are dealing with a criminal adventurer, and one who now has blood on his hands.' Herr Stern wiped his own hands. He said: 'Tomorrow, accredited copies of these documents will be provided, also communicated will be the findings of the investigation now in progress. These, added to your own case, should be sufficient to obtain a conviction. And I can only convey my great sadness that such a sordid affair should have occurred in your jurisdiction.'

157

He rose. He shook hands. He said: 'Just one more thing! Is it possible that, in this rural locality, one may obtain a good dinner?'

Gently pointed him to the Castle Arms.

Herr Stern shook hands again.

As he passed the limousine he threw a word to the chauffeur, who clicked his heels and got into the car.

'Coffee and sandwiches, I think. And then we'll have him back in.'

It was full dark now, and the mist had settled in the deserted square, though somewhere a watery moon was trying to lend a little illumination. Gently had sent refreshment out to the chauffeur, but the provident chauffeur had brought his own food. Refreshment had also been offered to the prisoner, who had angrily sent it away.

'A bit of a character, that Kraut, sir! I wonder what his missus thinks of him.'

Several times, during the preceding interview, Gently had caught the amused gleam in Aspall's eye. An element of farce! The local Inspector had found it hard to keep a straight face. Yet . . . if those exchanges had been in English, the drama underlying them exposed? For Schmeikel there had been no farce. He had learned that the last card was down. If before he had nursed hope of some avenue of escape, that hope was now dead. He was on his own. In Germany, In England, the prison door was yawning wide.

And meanwhile, behind closed curtains, in the yacht at the quay Trudi Schmeikel waited: perhaps more lonely than her husband, alone with her thoughts. With her fears. Did she know, or was she merely guessing? Gently pictured again that peaked, narrow face, the frightened eyes, the dishevelled locks, those sudden collapses into tears. What had Schmeikel told her when, at first dawn, he had insisted on getting the yacht under way? What excuse for disobeying the police injunction and flying from the place where his uncle had died? Surely then she must have guessed, if not before. No problems at home could have excused such an act. If they were escaping, it was from only one thing, and whether he had told her or not, she knew.

Gently ate his sandwiches, drank his coffee, thought of lighting his pipe, but didn't. He nodded to Aspall.

'Right.'

'The final act, sir?' Aspall said, rising.

'It looks like it.'

'Well, he's had a good run, sir. If it was down to me I would have done him sooner.'

Aspall left. Through the office window, Gently could see the chauffeur peering in at him. He got up, went to the window, and drew the two dusty curtains across it; then, after hesitating, those of a second window. Then he went back to his chair at the desk.

'You may smoke, Schmeikel.'

When the German entered it was plain that some of the defiance had evaporated. Without looking at Gently he advanced to the chair, sat, and remained staring at the desk. In his fulsome cheeks, a touch of pallor; some disarray in the bushy hair. Now he felt in his pocket and dropped on the desk a cigar case that was obviously empty. Gently shrugged.

'Would you care for coffee?'

He barely shook his head. He was sitting with his legs out straight and his hands clasped across his stomach. Gently regarded him for some moments. He said:

'I think you know the situation, Schmeikel. If there is anything you still wish to tell me, I am quite prepared to listen.'

159

'And then – to hear you tell me I am a liar?'

'I should warn you that our investigation has been thorough.'

'Oh yes, so thorough!' He dragged on his hands. 'And yet now you are seeking to trap me some more?'

'I am willing to listen.'

Schmeikel tossed his head. 'And I, I am not willing to go along! I say I am innocent, and then no more. Out of my own mouth you shall not destroy me.'

'You reaffirm that you are innocent.'

'*Gott im himmel*, yes! For what reason will I be killing my uncle?'

Gently paused. 'You wouldn't care to reconsider that?'

But Schmeikel had clamped his lips tight shut.

Gently shrugged. 'Very well, then! We will go over your statement one more time. I would like you to describe to me again the movements of yourself and your wife on Tuesday evening. Shall we say after dinner?'

At last Schmeikel looked at him, and fear was present in his stare. He snapped: 'I have said. For this, is no need. All, I have written down and signed.'

'For coffee, you went to the lounge, I believe.'

'Is no matter! Read what I say.'

'Where other guests were present?'

'I do not remember!'

'In your statement, they are mentioned.'

Schmeikel's mouth set tight again. Gently said: 'The Castle Arms lounge has access to the garden to enable guests to step outside. On an unclement night it is unlikely that any would, which would make the circumstance more easily remembered. We have spoken to the guests. To a certain lady. She recalled a couple of her neighbours who discoursed in German.'

'*Ach*, is no matter!'

'Did you go outside, Schmeikel?'

'I tell you no matter, is nothing at all.' He dragged on

the hands. 'Is Trudi, yes? She is feeling sick, is unwell. She wishes for air, so we step out. Why am I putting this in my statement?'

'You accompanied your wife?'

'I am saying.'

'And returned with her?'

'But yes!'

'Then together you left, and went down to the quay?'

'Is in my statement – why should I lie?'

Gently stared long. He said: 'Next to the garden is a passage or alleyway that leads into the square. From the garden there is access to it by a door which, for security reasons, is kept bolted at night. On Wednesday morning that door was found unbolted by the staff member whose care it is.'

'I cannot help this!'

'Did you unbolt that door, Schmeikel?'

'No. I do not see any door.'

'You didn't leave by that way?'

'*Ach*, how many times! We go out, we come in, we leave together. Is she not telling you?'

Gently shook his head. 'Your wife re-entered the hotel alone. For this we have a witness. You were not seen again after accompanying her into the garden.'

'Then you are being told lies!'

'And later, you were seen proceeding alone towards the quay.'

'Lies – more lies! That man is an informer. I think you are paying him to say these things.'

'But would we pay your wife?'

'Trudi – *ach*, you shall leave my wife alone! Trudi is good, poor little Trudi. She will not tell these lies of her husband.'

'Of her own movements she was obliged to give account.'

'Her movements, mine, these I am telling you.'

161

'Schmeikel, she joined you later. She met you returning from the quay.'

'Never – never! Why will she say this? All these things you tell me are untrue.'

And again Gently shook his head.

Schmeikel dragged on his hands. He stared at the desk. Sweat was beginning to reappear on his brow. But once more his mouth was set in a trap, his face grim with determination. Gently said:

'You left the hotel alone. Your wife was obliged to return to use the facilities. It would be approximately a quarter of an hour later when she left to rejoin you. In the meantime you had reached the quay, where your uncle had gone to await you. A witness saw him there minutes before you arrived. But when your wife joined you, your uncle was missing. These are the facts.'

'No – not the facts!'

Gently said: 'You maintain that the witnesses, your wife, are lying?'

'It is nothing, it does not matter!' At last the clenched hands were wrenched apart. 'Trudi, no, she tells no lies, but what then? Does it make me a killer?'

'Yet you lied about it.'

'*Ach, so*! A petty detail I do not tell you.'

'A detail so vital?'

'Is nothing, I say! All the rest I am telling you is true.'

'Schmeikel, you went alone to that place. You left the hotel by an obscure exit. You knew who was waiting for you there, and that the chances were there would be no witness. And a man died, a man who stood between you and enormous wealth. And we find you trying to conceal the critical fact that you went there alone. What shall we think?'

'Oh, *mein Gott*!' Schmeikel rocked in the chair. 'She is there so soon – is it not so? How am I to do this, and she know nothing?'

'It would not have taken long.'

'But yes, I say! It is minutes only till she is there. I go, I find no Gunther, I make my return to enquire at the ale-house. And she is meeting me there, where the road makes a hump, is no question but she must see all.'

'I repeat, it would not have taken long. A determined man could achieve the deed in seconds.'

'But tell me why – why am I doing this?'

Gently said: 'I don't think I need to tell you that.'

Schmeikel dashed sweat. 'It is because of these men – you are believing what they have to tell you?'

Gently stared at him, but said nothing. Schmeikel gazed with helpless eyes. Slowly, his two hands gripped together again, and his eyes fell to the desk.

'I deny everything, yes? There are no such matters as you are thinking. I leave Trudi behind because we are late, and Uncle Gunther likes all things punctual. There is no plotting and there is no planning. I have no reason to make away with my uncle. This thing has happened as you have been told, and I defy any man to prove different.'

It was quite a little speech and, for once, he was contriving to keep his eyes fixed on Gently's. But the gripped hands were trembling and having to be kept pressed close to his body. Gently said:

'Yet your uncle died.'

'Then it is the peasants you should be seeking! Or an accident, perhaps, yes? A drunk old man falling into the river?'

'Your uncle had been attacked, Schmeikel.'

'This you assume. You cannot know.'

Gently shook his head. 'The bruises tell the story. Bruises inflicted only shortly before death.'

'But . . . he is from a yacht! It is common to have such bruises. I myself – and perhaps Trudi – !'

163

'No, Schmeikel.'

'Then a quarrel at the inn – '

'No.'

'You do not know this!'

'We know.'

'*Ach, Gott mir helfen!*' His staring eyes fell back to the desk. He said: 'Is the business, yes? I am killing him for that? They tell you all these things, and you are saying it is why I do it?'

Gently was silent.

'Yes, is why! And now, no Uncle to say different. I am alone to face my enemies, who are wishing me made a killer. Is it not for this that they come to you, with their papers, their accusations? Oh yes! And you are believing them, all is now so easy for the English *polizei*. I am there, I have such reasons – pouf! One hundred years in an English jail.'

Gently said: 'You claim to be innocent of their allegations?'

He hugged his hands. 'You will call me a liar! Without Uncle Gunther, no witness that I do these things with honest purpose. And is a reason to kill him, yes? That I am left with no answer to what shall be alleged? It is not the logic, I am no such fool. Why will I be killing my Uncle Gunther?'

'In fact, the transfer of funds was of honest intent?'

'Yes, but how to prove this, in an English prison? My enemies will triumph unopposed, and Willi Schmeikel be branded a villain. *Ach*!' He thumped his hands on his knees. 'Perhaps is best you convict me here. Then, a fair sentence, with reductions, yes? While at home I may never walk free again.'

Gently stared. 'It that a confession?'

Schmeikel hesitated, perhaps a little too long. '*Gott*, no! But I will stand my trial, and there swear me the innocent man that I am.'

'The innocent man.'

'Yes, I say!'

Gently said: 'A confession may help to lighten the sentence.'

He shook his head. 'No. No. I take that chance. It may be yet that your jury may believe me.'

'To a charge you will plead innocence.'

'Yes, I say.' His mouth twisted. 'You are hearing me,' he said. 'And so?'

Gently looked him over, the sweating forehead, the pallid cheeks, the drooping mouth. He said: 'First I shall require you to amend your statement, to include the admissions you have just made.'

'To amend . . .?' Schmeikel stared. 'And then, after I do this, you charge me?'

'After you have done that, you will be allowed a little time to consider your position.'

'But – I am telling you!'

'A little time. Also, I think, you should talk to your wife. We will arrange to have her fetched, and for your meeting to be in private. Is that agreeable?'

Schmeikel's eyes were popping. 'You are thinking, perhaps, that she – !'

'Is it agreeable?'

'*Ach*, very well! But do not, for one moment, think – '

Gently nodded to the grim-faced Aspall, who rose and touched Schmeikel's shoulder. Trance-like, Schmeikel got off his chair, stared a moment, then allowed Aspall to prod him towards the door. But there he hesitated, looking back at Gently. He faltered:

'Trudi . . . if it is permitted . . .?'

'Yes?'

'In the yacht . . . cigars . . .'

Gently nodded. Then Aspall led Schmeikel away.

*

'I really can't see any point, sir, in hanging it out longer. The DPP will have to rubber-stamp this one.'

Aspall was back, his face no less grim, and apparently too agitated to sit down. He stood staring at Gently, who had at last got a pipe going, and sat toying with the cigar container Schmeikel had left behind.

'I was watching him all the time, sir. He's as guilty as hell, and it showed. And I'll bet his wife knows it too, and he's as scared as the devil she's going to drop something. Why don't we just charge him and get it over?'

Gently blew a smoke ring. 'You're probably right!'

'We could have him back at Eastwich tonight, sir, and in front of a magistrate in the morning.'

Gently nodded. 'Yet he was right about one thing.'

'Then I must have missed it, sir!'

Gently said: 'A live uncle might well have helped him out of his troubles back home.'

'That wouldn't have stopped him.'

'There's a chance that it might. I don't think the situation would be lost on him. If what was going on there was close to the wind, it would need the both of them to face it out.'

'So it was a risk, and he had to take it, and now he's on his own with all that dough.'

Gently shrugged. 'Schmeikel is no fool. And he probably isn't a poor man in any case.'

'But, with all we've got on him, sir!'

'It's a case, of course. Just, one is left wondering about the man. What led him into an action so suicidal, and which could only end up in one way. Could there be an angle we haven't hit on?'

Aspall wriggled his shoulders frustratedly. 'I'm through with angles!' he said. 'We've got all we need on Schmeikel, no call to be hunting up fresh ones.'

'Still – before we take the plunge.' Gently blew another

ring. 'Perhaps one more session with our principal witness – he still has a question or two to answer.'

'You mean Stratton, sir?'

Gently nodded. 'I think I'll call on the man at home. And meanwhile you can have a pint at the Mariners, to check any improvements in Shavers' memory.'

Aspall stared hard. 'You can't really believe, sir . . .?'

'After that, we come back to Schmeikel.'

'Yes, sir. Schmeikel,' Aspall said plangently. 'And I hope they've got a cell aired back in Eastwich!'

11

Night-flying was in progress at RAF Buxhall. Gently had taken the inland route, to find, as he progressed, the mist growing thinner, and then disappearing altogether as river and marshes were left behind. The route skirted the airfield. From a modest eminence it brought into view the principal runway, its boundaries dusted with ghostly points of light, with other lights sparkling in the remote distance. Gently drew into the verge for a moment, where other cars had parked before him. He could hear the bellow of far-off engines being run and see movements in the distant lights. Then, suddenly, an echoing thunder of sound, and lights that were accelerating towards him, a black, menacing shape, expanding as though by magic, at the last moment leaping and flashing by over his head . . . in fifty years, had very much changed? In those days, fewer lights, on most nights none. While the black shapes, Lancs, Halifaxes, would have laboured more desperately to gain the skies . . .

He glanced in the other direction, at the fields, the dark trees. Grange Farm must lie almost in the flight-path of the bombers taking off from Buxhall. Night after night they would have heard them go over, engines straining to make height, straining to lift the deadly loads destined for the Ruhr, Bremen, Berlin. Willum, still in his forties: the young Jimmy: the Land Girl, Mabs; and Molly, ambitious

Molly, whose officer-lover was guiding part of that thunder. Ozzie, who wasn't Robert. And whose letters had begun to sound plaintive . . .

Gently shrugged and drove on. One angle too many, lost in a past not to be recovered, some letters in an attic. Beside what they had, why brood on it further?

He kept to the main road and drove as directly as possible to Wolmering. Stratton's apartment was on the front, in a terrace facing the sea. He found the terrace; close behind it the town's lighthouse was flashing its measured signals, while down the coast one saw the sparkle of lights that denoted the atomic power station: Gabrielle's 'St Satan's'. Gently parked, locked up the car and crossed the road to number 34. He didn't have to ring. As he mounted the steps, the door opened, and Stratton stood before him.

'Were you going out?'

'I – no!'

Gently had asked, because this evening Stratton was wearing a suit, a smart though sombre two-piece, along with a knitted waistcoat and a tie. His more familiar anorak could be seen hanging from a peg in the hall.

'You were perhaps expecting someone?'

'No – I told you! I would be here the whole evening. I just saw your car pull up, and I thought I would save you the trouble of ringing. Do come in!'

He stepped back to allow Gently to enter, then closed the door after him and pointed the way into a lounge. Gently went in curiously. It was a room with a faintly old-fashioned feel to it, its carpet, furnishings of yesteryear, a wallpaper that suggested the fifties. On its walls hung bird studies by Roland Green, and bird books occupied a bureau-bookcase. Among trinkets on the mantelpiece was

169

a framed photograph of a girl, a print in grained mono-
tone. Gently went to study it. But the girl was a blonde
and exhibited no sign of a kiss-curl.

'An old girlfriend?'

'My – sister, actually! She's widowed now and lives in
Brighton. Why do you ask?'

Gently shrugged, and fingered a badge lying on a china
tray.

'A war memento . . .'

'Yes, what else. I wore it, and I'm not ashamed.'

'Do you still have your uniform?'

'How did you guess?'

Gently's shoulders moved again.

'Look, let's sit down!' Stratton exclaimed agitatedly.
'You've come for something, I know that. I stayed in
specially. Is it to tell me you've made up your mind about
the nephew?'

'He is still helping us.'

'But does that mean . . .'

'It means exactly that,' Gently said.

'Oh, do sit down!' Stratton exclaimed. He himself
plumped down on a winged armchair. 'I've been reading
the evening paper and listening to the radio, and they all
seem certain that the nephew is guilty. Of course, I didn't
like the fellow. He bullied that wife of his terribly. But can
you really be so sure, and must I stand up and give
testimony against him?'

Gently wandered over to the bay window, across which
curtains had not been drawn. Out there the moon made a
pathway in the sea, and far off one could see the faint
lights of some ship. He said:

'You feel some doubt about his guilt?'

'Yes . . . perhaps. I don't know! But it would be a
terrible thing to give testimony while feeling he was
innocent, after all. I mean, we don't know. I merely saw
him on his way there. He may well be as innocent as he

170

claims. Anything could have happened to that man after I left and before the nephew got there. It could, couldn't it?'

'In – such a short time?'

'Yes! He could have slipped off that bollard.'

Gently stared at the sea. 'But there were bruises,' he said.

'But they could have happened . . .!'

Gently shook his head.

'Then . . . there's no doubt. Is that what you're telling me?'

'No doubt that Herschfeldt was attacked.'

'And . . . it has to be the nephew?'

Gently stared at the sea.

'Oh lord,' Stratton murmured. 'Oh lord!'

To the sea, Gently said: 'On another topic. This concerns the war and your time at Buxhall.'

'No, I don't want to talk about that!' Stratton burst out. 'It isn't a time I wish to remember.'

Gently said: 'You may be able to help. I wish to locate an officer who served there. He was at Buxhall at the same time as yourself. A pilot. His first name was Osbert.'

'But – why do you want to know about him?'

'Then you knew him?' Gently said.

'Yes, I knew him! Everybody did. But what has that got to do with all this?'

'If you would just tell me what you remember.'

'Oh, all right, then – if I must!' Reflected in the window-pane, Gently saw Stratton staring at the carpet between his feet. 'Ozzie Fowler. He was a pain. His wife had run off with a Yank. He was putting in for a divorce, and everyone had to be told about it. But the fact is, and everyone knew it, he was just as bad as she was. He had to keep it dark, of course, but he'd got someone else on the side.' Stratton's head jerked. 'Anything else?'

171

Gently nodded to the sea. 'Are you still in touch with him?'

'In touch . . . how could I be! He went for a Burton not long after that.'

'You mean he was killed?'

'Yes.'

'He – died on a raid?'

Stratton's head shook impatiently. 'He pranged a kite on a test flight. It was the next summer, when I was in France. A mate of mine got a letter from his wife. Fowler's kite had been in the hangar for inspection, and he took it up to do a circuit and bump. When he landed the undercart folded and the kite cartwheeled and blew up.'

'He was killed instantly?'

'Of course.'

'And that was in the summer of . . .'45?'

'When I was in France, yes. But I can't think why you'd be interested in him.'

Gently went on staring at the sea. The lights of the ship on the horizon had grown more distinct. Almost certainly it would be the ferry from The Hook treading its familiar course towards Harwich. But the moon, on the other hand, seemed to have paled, was casting a frailer light on the waters.

'Why – why are we talking about this?' Stratton faltered. His eyes were on the photograph in the frame: on the woman who wasn't Molly Hardyment.

Gently shrugged, and turned from the window.

'Let's get back to Sunday at the reserve. You saw the Hardyments there, of course?'

'The Hardyments . . . ?'

'Yes. I understand they were out at The Pulk at the same time as you.'

'Oh . . . yes. I think I did see them there. Yes, I did, now you come to mention it.'

Gently had taken a chair, not quite opposite Stratton,

but from which he still had the window and the sea in view. The nervous ex-bank man also kept his eyes averted, staring now at the window, now at the floor. He was trying to keep his posture relaxed, sitting half-reclined in the wing-chair, but the movements of his hands, his head, were jerky as he answered the questions put to him.

'I believe you've known them a long time.'

'Yes. I suppose so! But only since I moved to the branch here. And then, for years, it was simply as customers. It's only recently I've known them through the bird society.'

'During the war, of course . . .?'

'No, I told you! You can ask them if you don't believe me.'

'You perhaps made other acquaintances.'

'Perhaps. Some.'

'You'd be meeting girls.'

'Look – ! Must we?' Now he did turn pleading eyes on Gently, his creased mouth working.

'Say – just one?'

'I won't talk about it! I've told you all you need to know.' He jerked his head away, stared at the window, his lank jaw set in a tight line.

Gently said: 'Very well, then. Getting back to the reserve on Sunday. I believe that, following your visit to The Pulk, you sought refreshment in the coffee room.'

'Do – they say that?'

Gently said nothing.

'All right – if you must!' Stratton said. 'Yes, I went there, I usually do. I sat at my usual table by the window.'

'Then you would have seen the Hardyments and their friend.'

'Yes, I suppose so. If they saw me.'

'You saw him approach their table, witnessed their mutual recognition, heard the excited conversation that followed.'

173

'I – don't admit that!' But his voice was quavering. 'Look, I really wasn't paying that much attention. My mind was elsewhere, on the egret, the migration. If anything, I was wishing they wouldn't be so noisy.'

Gently stared out at the sea. 'I think you are lying to me.' he said. 'You did hear, Stratton. You heard Herschfeldt's story. You knew who that man was when you met him outside. Isn't that so?'

'But, if I'd had the slightest idea – !'

'You knew that man was Gunther Herschfeldt.'

'Yes, I may have heard the name!'

'Yet, later, you denied it.'

'It's just – it's just that I didn't think it important!'

'Not – important?'

'Please . . . believe me!' Stratton extended a wavering hand. 'I know it must sound suspicious to you, but honestly I didn't think it mattered. I was so mixed up with this business – I – I didn't want to get mixed up any further. So I was just saying as little as I could. But if I'd thought it was important . . .'

Gently shook his head at the sea.

'You believe me, don't you?'

Gently said nothing.

'Oh lord, well it's up to you!' Stratton said. 'Of course, you don't take anything at face value.'

Gently turned to look at him. Stratton stared back desperately. 'You knew who that man was,' Gently said. 'When you met him outside. When you accompanied him. When something mysterious took place, down by the stream. Was that so unimportant, too?'

'Yes – it was, if you'll only believe me!'

'Herschfeldt thought you were trying to steal his camera.'

'You know, you must know, that that's untrue!'

'So what did happen?'

174

'He simply turned on me. There was no rhyme or reason in it. He seemed to be wanting to get rid of me, and started shoving me away.'

'The violence initiated with him?'

'Yes. Yes. I couldn't understand it.'

'And ceased when some other people arrived?'

'If you could find them, I'm sure they'd tell you!'

Gently turned back to the sea again. 'Something else you heard in the coffee room,' he said. 'The arrangements for Tuesday. Where Herschfeldt might be found. An opportunity to meet with him again.'

Stratton's voice was tremulous. 'I – I give up!' he said. 'Now everything you're going to use against me. I swear I heard nothing of any arrangements. It was pure coincidence, me being at Harford.'

'Just . . . the autumn migration.'

'Yes. Oh, I know it means nothing to you! But to me, it's a lifetime study, the thing that's always kept me going. Birds are my life. I can't expect you to understand, you probably have other interests, people. But I'm alone. The birds are my family. Without them, I don't think I could exist.'

'The birds are your family . . .'

'Yes.'

'Replacing people. A wife.'

'A . . . did you have to say that?'

Gently stared at him. Stratton hung his head.

'So,' Gently said. 'A complete coincidence. You watched birds, had dinner, drove down to the quay. On a foggy inclement night you spent – how long was it? – an hour down there?'

'Oh, it's just useless!' Stratton flung round to face the window. 'I might have known. It's all my fault. I'm only in this mess because I spoke up.'

'You waited. But was it only for the birds?'

175

'Tell me, how could I know I was going to see him? Even suppose I knew where he was, the odds were he'd be staying at the hotel.'

'So you took that risk.'

'This is just impossible!'

'And the risk paid off. Herschfeldt came there alone. Not the stranger of your statement, but Gunther Herschfeldt, ex-POW and former resident at Grange Farm. The man you had met on Sunday, and between whom and yourself there had been violence.'

'And I told you what happened!'

'So tell me again.'

'It's pointless – pointless!' He rocked in the chair.

After a pause, Gently rose and went across to the mantelpiece. He picked up the framed photograph of the blonde girl, a smiling girl in a velour dress. The frame belonged to another era: stamped, gilded metal, with the gilding dulled, while the monochrome print on its matt-surface paper showed a hint of browning at the edges. Gently held it out to Stratton.

'This isn't your sister, is it?' he said.

'Oh, please . . . no!'

'Was she a girlfriend?'

'No – no!'

'Perhaps . . . your wife?'

Stratton rocked. He plunged his face in his hands. He was trying to hold back sobs. At last he got out:

'It's no good, is it? All this . . . it's just going through the motions!'

'Was she your wife?'

'I knew you'd come for me! I've been waiting, ever since . . .'

'And . . . somehow . . . she met him?'

'Oh God, no! How can you even begin to think . . .?' He dragged his hands from his streaming eyes. 'Josie . . . she'd never have looked at another man! She and I were meant for each other. She was the only one, the only woman. The only woman in the world . . .'

'Then . . .?'

He scrubbed at his eyes. 'Over there – on Sunday. Yes, I was listening to every word! Who he was, why he was there, and the date – the date when he was shot down.'

Gently said: 'The date?'

'The date I shall never forget in this life! 21st October 1944. The date they'll find written on my heart!'

'The date he was shot down . . .?'

'Give me her picture!'

Gently gave it him. He hugged it to his breast.

'Is there some brandy in this cabinet?'

The groaning Stratton managed to nod. Gently found the bottle, poured out a glass, and stood holding it out to Stratton. At first it seemed he meant to ignore it and to go on hugging the picture; but at last he lowered the picture to his knees and received the glass in a shaky hand. He sipped a very little. He wasn't looking at Gently. His bleared eyes seemed to be staring at a different world. Gently moved to the window, stood looking out, waiting. At last he heard Stratton set down the glass. Stratton said:

'She – she . . . we'd just had the news from the MO. I'd have been a father! Perhaps, now . . .' He grabbed the glass and drank more brandy.

Gently said: 'Your wife was living in?'

'Yes . . . living in. And she'd only been there since June! At first – we were married in '43 – we rented a bungalow near her folks. But then . . . it wasn't any life, just seeing her on leave or a forty-eight. I spoke to the CO, and he was agreeable. So when a vacancy occurred in married quarters . . .' His head sank. 'She wanted it too – I can't blame myself entirely! In her letters she was always asking me, and when she got there it seemed like heaven.'

177

'In June of '44.'

'Yes. June. Even the weather was fine that year. We used to go on rambles – she was fond of birds, too – rambles on the marshes and in the forest. I can remember . . . but never mind! None of that counts for anything now.'

'Five happy months.'

'Please – don't! I can't bear to remember how short it was.' He dashed at his eyes. 'Even that autumn. The colours can never be as fine again.'

Gently said: 'Of course you weren't on leave, as you told me.'

He closed his eyes tight. 'No. Not then. But it was due. On the very next day. That night I had the pass and the warrants in my pocket, we were catching a train from Beckford in the morning. First we were going to visit her people, then we had a room booked in Torquay. We were packed, ready. I'd rung MT, had transport booked to the station.'

'You – were on duty that night?'

'Bloody duty officer.' The eyes were still screwed tight. 'At six I was due at Admin. Five minutes to six. The last time I saw her. During the evening I rang her twice, the last time just before eleven. Then I was due to inspect the guard on dispersal, myself, driver and NCO.' His mouth was trembling. 'A night like tonight, a full moon, a bit of mist. We weren't really expecting him again, though Fighter Command had been advised.'

'A bomber's moon.'

'Don't. There'd been some activity earlier on. Some of ours going over, the usual thing. We'd had no alerts. We drove out, stopped at the guard-hut. That – that was where we heard the siren.'

'It – was him?'

'Oh God!' Stratton covered his face. 'The siren was still sounding when the first one fell. Then the second. The corporal shouted, ' "I think he's got HQ, sir!" We got back

178

in the car and drove like mad, but soon we could see he'd missed HQ. The smoke was coming from somewhere else. The corporal shouted, "Oh lor', he's hit officers' quarters!" Stratton shuddered uncontrollably.

'Finish the brandy,' Gently said.

'I can't – I can't go on! I don't have to tell you the rest.'

'Still – finish it.'

In desperation, Stratton seized the glass and tossed off the contents. It set him choking, and Gently had to move fast to field the sliding photograph. He set it aside, face down, on a table at a distance from Stratton. In a little, Stratton recovered himself, sat panting and staring at nothing. Gently said quietly:

'Did you see her again?'

Stratton shook his head. 'They wouldn't let me. Said it was better if I didn't.' He shuddered again. 'They – they took her straight off to the mortuary. That was next day, when they cleared the rubble. All they let me see was the coffin.'

'Did you know the aircraft had been shot down?'

'The whole station knew, there were celebrations in the mess. I tried to find out about the pilot, but of course they wouldn't tell me that. Until . . . until Sunday, I thought the pilot had died in the crash.'

'Until Sunday.'

Stratton said nothing.

'Then you knew,' Gently said. 'The man who had killed your wife and child was alive, was sitting a couple of tables away.'

'When I heard the date . . . I knew.'

'And on that same date, Gunther Herschfeldt died.'

'Yes . . . he died.' Stratton turned his head to gaze at the now upturned picture lying on the table.

*

179

Gently said: 'I should warn you. You are not obliged to answer further questions. On the other hand, we are here without a witness, which would enable you to deny any statement you may make now. Do you understand, Stratton?'

He dragged his gaze from the picture. 'Does that make any difference . . . now?'

'Perhaps very little,' Gently shrugged. 'But I wish you to understand.'

'I understand.' He straightened himself slightly, raised his watery eyes to Gently's. 'I knew you were coming,' he said. 'I knew it would have to end like this. I couldn't have gone through with it, you charging the other fellow, me having to tell my lies against him.' His mouth worked. He said: 'I've got a bag packed. I'm ready.'

Gently said: 'Do you want to tell me more?'

'More . . .?'

'Say on the Sunday. What was your intention?'

Stratton stared. 'I . . . don't know,' he said. 'Suddenly . . . I felt! And then I struck him. But I don't know. And then the people came.' He paused. 'I felt ashamed,' he said. 'Afterwards. And yet . . . I knew where I could find him again. I couldn't get it out of my mind.' He paused again. 'Perhaps I wanted to apologise. At least, I had to see him again!'

'So, on Tuesday?'

'I went . . . you know. At first I wasn't certain I'd even go in to Harford. I was on the Thwaite marshes most of the day, trying to keep my mind on the birds. Only I couldn't. I kept remembering that down there, down the river . . . And always, after a day on those marshes, I would finish up with dinner at the Arms.' He looked away. 'I'd gone there with Josie. Twice. Oh, I know I was a fool!'

Gently said: 'At the Arms, you would see the Schmeikels.'

180

Stratton nodded. 'I thought at first there'd been a change of plan. I knew who they were, of course, I'd seen them with him in the coffee room. I was on edge, expecting him to arrive, and then he'd see me and demand explanations. But he didn't arrive, and as dinner went ahead I realised he wasn't going to.'

'He was at the Mariners.'

'Yes. And even then I wasn't sure . . .'

'Did you look in there?'

'I can't explain it! I felt I had to see him, once more.'

'So?'

Stratton stared ahead. 'The other two cleared off to the lounge. I drank my coffee, paid, sat in my car. But at last I drove down there.'

'To the quay?'

'Yes. Where I parked this morning. Then . . . then I got out and strolled back to the pub. It was noisy, the music was playing. I looked through the window. I saw him.'

'You didn't go in.'

'How could I? He'd have been on to me in a moment. And I couldn't explain . . . not there, with everything that was going on. It was him who was playing the concertina, and the rest had got the tables back, dancing. And there'd clearly been a lot of drinking. I don't think many of them were sober.'

'He looked . . . a happy man?'

'He . . . he wasn't drunk. Not playing the concertina like that. He looked . . .' Stratton's head bowed. 'Yes . . . he looked a happy man.'

Gently said: 'How long did you stay there?'

'Oh, not long. A couple of minutes. I was scared of being seen. I just wanted to be sure that he was there. Then I cleared off back to the car.'

'To – wait for him.'

'I can't be certain! I could just as easily have driven straight home. But yes, I thought there was a possibility

181

. . . I knew the other two weren't with him. Then that fellow turned up. He really seemed furtive, seemed to be wanting me to go, and of course I didn't. And after him . . . there really were birds coming over, you know!'

Gently said: 'You had no settled intention.'

'Just . . . that I wanted him on his own.'

'No more than that.'

'No. No more.'

'And so you waited. And he arrived.'

Stratton looked at the brandy glass. Gently made no motion. Stratton turned away and stared at the wall. He said: 'I didn't mean it. I simply didn't. It just happened . . . I shall never know how.'

'You got out to speak to him?'

'Yes. He was sitting on the bollard, humming this tune. He smiled as he saw me get out and come over to him. And then – suddenly – his appearance changed. He jumped up, took a step towards me, and threw up his fists like a boxer. He was going to strike me, I couldn't help it. I had to put up mine too.'

'You didn't speak to him?'

'There was no time!'

'He initiated the attack?'

'If only someone will believe me! I never had the chance to explain.'

'Of course, he had recognised you.'

'He must have. He must have thought I was after him again. But I wasn't. I was going to apologise, or at least explain what it was about. Simply, there wasn't time. He was on me, and I had to handle it as best I could.'

'So . . . take me through it.'

'I cant! He was hitting me, and I was hitting him.'

'But . . . ?'

Stratton was staring hard into nowhere. 'I think . . . the bollard. He must have backed into it.'

'He backed into the bollard.'

'Yes . . . he must have! I struck him, and he backed into that.'

'You struck him.'

'He was striking me! I caught him in the chest, and he backed away.'

'And – then?'

Stratton clasped his head. 'I know – I know I should have done something about it! But I didn't realise what had happened to him, I was simply relieved to have got clear.'

'He went into the river.'

'I didn't know! There was a ladder, rungs, he could have climbed out. And then he would have attacked me again. I didn't know he'd hit his head on something.'

'You didn't stop to ascertain.'

'No! I'd had enough trouble, I wanted to get out. I thought he might be waiting down there to grab me, so I just ran back to the car and cleared off.'

'Leaving Herschfeldt to drown.'

'Oh God, if you like. But I didn't know that. I didn't know!'

'The man who had killed your wife and child.'

Stratton gave a deep groan, and hugged his head.

Now Gently did refill the glass, and thrust it into Stratton's trembling hand. Stratton stared at it, but didn't drink. At last his eyes found Gently's again. He said:

'So . . . what happens now?'

'You will see the magistrate in the morning,' Gently said.

'And then . . .?'

'Bail may be possible. But perhaps you should bring that bag.'

Stratton's eyes switched to the up-turned picture, then back to Gently. Gently nodded.

'I think that will be allowed,' he said. 'Just stick it in your bag.'

Stratton drank some of the brandy. Then he rose shakily and went to fetch the bag. Gently remained staring out of the window, at the moonlit sea, the flashes of light from the lighthouse. A bomber's moon. And down the coast the skimming lights of an aircraft. From the airfield, fifty years later. The airfield where some had died.

'I'm ready.'

To the suit, Stratton had added a coat and trilby. But at the last moment he remembered the heating system, and had to return to switch it off.

12

Schmeikel had been right about one thing: the gales of autumn were close at hand. Barely twenty-four hours later a force 8 south-westerly was flogging the yachts still remaining on the moorings. The North Sea had become a raging wilderness of towering waves and blinding spray, swept by squalls of rain and gusts rising to forces 9 and 10. Fortunately, the *Electra* had not made sail. The German Embassy had put its spoke in: Schmeikel and his tearful wife had been shepherded to a flight from Heathrow, and the *Electra* left on moorings to await some subsequent disposition.

'It still smells.' The AC could barely accept the turn events had taken. 'I mean, honestly, Gently, can we really credit the confession that fellow made? That business with his wife is ancient history, normally one wouldn't give it a second look. And Schmeikel has got about everything going for him – even his own people can't believe he's innocent!'

'I'm afraid the facts support the charge, sir.'

'Gently, it smells. Are you certain that Schmeikel didn't get at the fellow?'

'I can't quite see how, sir.'

'Then think about it! And remember the sort of pressure that Schmeikel could have put on him. A million or two was nothing to Schmeikel, but it would have seemed like the earth to, what's his name, Stratton. And the odds are, with such a tale, he'll have the jury in tears, and get away with a suspended sentence at most. Have you thought about that?'

Gently shrugged to himself. 'I'm afraid the facts rule out collusion, sir.'

'Then damn the facts! This case smells. And I trusted you to get to the bottom of it, Gently.'

Aspall too had been difficult to convince that Stratton could credibly be accepted as the culprit. At the first opportunity he had taken Gently aside and blurted out his objections.

'Look, sir, we've seen it all before – and Stratton's just the sort of bloke to try it on! He's in it for the kicks, to get his name in print, and then he'll swear blind he confessed under duress. We can't buy it. If we let Schmeikel go, we'll never lay hands on him a second time . . .'

'I think his Embassy means to take care of Schmeikel.'

Less incredulous were the Hardyments, on whom Gently had called on his way home to Heatherings. It was late, and the whole family were gathered together around a fire in the parlour – Willum, Jimmy, Mabs, Cynthy, Nellie and the earnest young Mark.

'Come you in and find a seat – Markie, run and fetch the man a drink!'

Ensconced by the hearth, with a pint in his hand, he had advised them of the latest development, of the events of long ago at the airfield from which planes were yet exercising overhead. Silently they heard him, pipes going, Cynthy with knitting lying on her lap. At last old Willum knocked out his pipe.

'Ah,' he said. 'Ah. But nothing to do with our Molly that wasn't. Though you was on the right track, old partner.'

'I always wondered about him,' Mabs said. 'Living all alone there, the way he did. You didn't find out who she was?'

'He come from Eastwich,' Jimmy said. 'Like as not she'd come from there too.'

'Could have met her anywhere, Jimmy.'

'Josie,' Jimmy said. 'Never knew a Josie. Not around here.'

'Perhaps she was from Shinglebourne.'

'Well there you are.'

'I knew a Josie once,' Cynthy said. 'But she married a postman, out Grimchurch way.'

Gently drank. He said: 'Your Molly.' He told them what he had learned from Stratton. Willum listened with his eyes squeezed tight, the others with theirs staring at the burning coals.

'So . . . like that . . .'

Gently nodded.

'Then it never was on account of old Gunther . . .?'

'I think that is certain.'

'Oh blast!' Willum said. 'If only she'd said something . . . if only she had.'

Gently said: 'The letters may provide a clue. I think most likely they planned to get married. But clearly the liaison had to be kept quiet if he was to succeed in his divorce. And then came the complication you know about. And finally that tragic accident at the airfield.'

'And all this time . . .'

'I was sure,' Jimmy said. 'Sure it was all along of Gunther!'

'So now you know,' Mabs said. 'You know how wrong you can be.'

'But . . .!'

Willum gazed at the coals. 'And she never said nothing,' he said. 'Not to her mother. Not to me. She just went ahead . . . up there.'

'Oh, don't you take on!' Mabs hurried to him and slipped her arm round his shoulders. 'There was a war on, and these things happened, no use going on about it now. You've still got us. Cynthy, put the kettle on!'

187

'Never a word,' Willum said.

'Well, it wasn't old Gunther,' Mabs said. 'And that's a bit of comfort for you, anyway.'

Willum pushed her arm away. 'And he's another one,' he said.

Gently finished his pint and left. At Heatherings, he was in time to catch the call from Gabrielle. She sounded excited. She said:

'My dear, it's all over the papers here this morning! He is dying, this Luftwaffe hero, just in time to escape a financial scandal. Is it not so – a scandal so big that beside it the Maxwell affair is peanuts? You are told about this? Here, they are certain that his nephew arranged the killing!'

Gently explained.

'Then – not the nephew?'

'Just a rather pathetic elderly man.'

'My dear, you will disappoint *Le Figaro*, and all the other Paris papers! It is just a personal thing, then – no connection?'

'No connection with the Herschfeldt millions.'

'Ha, that is a pity. Already I begin to feel myself losing interest. But just a sad old man?'

'A man who loves birds.'

'Oh yes! Such a one I can imagine. But tomorrow I am home, my dear, and then we can talk about these things. You are well?'

Gently hung up, and lit himself a last pipe. The morrow was Friday, and he was staying on at Heatherings. He felt he had earned himself the weekend.

Brundall, 1993–4

188